The Moment He Touched Her, She Felt A Familiar Shiver Run Down Her Spine.

Every single overworked nerve ending in her body lit up with awareness. Her chest tightened; her hand involuntarily gripped his to maintain the connection it craved.

His touches, however brief or fleeting, were better than any morphine drip. Just the brush of his fingers against her skin made her feel alive and tingly in a way totally inappropriate for someone in her present condition. It had been that way since the first time he'd pressed a soft kiss against the back of her hand. She might not know him by sight, but her body certainly recognized her lover. The pleasurable current cut through everything—the pain, the medication, the confusion.

If only she reacted that way to a man who liked her.

But when Will looked at her, she knew that no matter what had gone wrong between them, he felt that shiver, too.

Dear Reader,

You have no idea how long I've waited to write this letter to you, because it means that you're reading my very first book! The past year has been a life-changing whirlwind culminating in the pages you're holding in your hand. Thanks for coming along for the ride.

You get only one first book, and I'm thrilled that mine is Adrienne and Will's story. Some books are easier to write than others, and from the first moment this story popped into my head—oddly enough at 5:30 in the morning while I worked out on an elliptical machine at the gym—it was a joy to work on. The characters immediately came to life, and the words just flowed. From the beginning, I knew this special story would be "the one."

I can't wait for you to read Adrienne and Will's story and all the books that follow it. If you enjoy it, tell me by visiting my website at www.andrealaurence.com, like my fan page on Facebook, or follow me on Twitter. I'd love to hear from my readers! (*Wow, I have *readers.*)

Enjoy!

Andrea

ANDREA LAURENCE

has been a lover of reading and writing stories since she learned her ABCs. She always dreamed of seeing her work in print and is thrilled to finally be able to share her books with the world. A dedicated West Coast girl transplanted into the deep South, she's working on her own "happily ever after" with her boyfriend and their collection of animals that shed like nobody's business. You can contact Andrea at her website, www.andrealaurence.com.

I've spent weeks trying to decide who to dedicate
my first book to. It's not as easy as you think,
especially when you have so many wonderful, supportive
people in your life. There will be more books and more
dedications, but this book would simply not exist without—

My Mother, Meg
For telling me my whole life that
I could do anything I put my mind to, and believing it.

My Boyfriend, Jason
For watching motocross and football with his headset on
so I can write, and thinking chili dogs and takeout are better
than a gourmet, four-course meal cooked at home.

*And the Playfriends—Kira Sinclair, Kimberly Lang,
Dani Wade and Marilyn Puett*
For reading countless manuscript drafts, correcting
my grammatical shortcomings, plotting in hot tubs and
believing in me all those times I didn't believe in myself.

Prologue

"I am never taking this airline again. Do you know how much I paid for this ticket? Absolutely ridiculous!"

The sharp shriek of a woman's voice attacked Adrienne's ears the moment she stepped onto the plane and rounded the corner to first class. The woman sounded like she felt—although Adrienne was furious with herself, not a helpless flight attendant. She was going home a failure, but she had no one else to blame.

Her aunt told her that taking her father's life-insurance money to start a fashion-design company in Manhattan was a stupid, reckless thing to do. She'd be back in Milwaukee and broke within a year, she insisted.

At least her aunt wasn't right on all accounts. It had been nearly *three* years since she left. Adrienne had some moderate success, a few dedicated customers, but in the end, the cost of keeping afloat in New York City was more than she could take without a big break, and it never came.

Adrienne looked down at her boarding pass and started

eyeing the seat numbers for 14B as the line finally began to move. As she moved closer, she came to the horrible realization that the screamer was going to be her seatmate for the flight. The woman had finally calmed down, but she didn't look happy. Adrienne grabbed her book, stowed her bag in the overhead compartment and quickly took her seat, avoiding eye contact.

"I can't believe I got bumped from first class by a group of Japanese businessmen and crammed into the window seat. I can barely move my arms."

This was going to be the longest two hours of Adrienne's life. "Would you like to trade seats?" she asked. It was the one thing she could offer to save herself. As much as she would love to shove the woman up to first class, there were no seats unless she was amenable to sitting in the pilot's lap.

The little concession made a huge difference. "That would be wonderful, thank you." The woman's expression instantly softened and Adrienne could finally appreciate how attractive she was. A bad temper did little for her appearance. She smiled wide, revealing perfect white teeth and full lips, and for a moment she reminded Adrienne of her mother. They looked a lot alike, with long, straight, shiny dark brown hair and bright green eyes. She could be Adrienne's attractive, put-together older sister, really. Her suit was expensive and impeccably tailored. Her shoes were this season's hottest Jimmy Choos.

Adrienne suppressed a sudden pang of jealousy. This woman was better suited to be the beautiful and fabulous Miriam Lockhart's only daughter. Adrienne inherited her mother's fondness for fashion and skill with a sewing machine, but physically, she had more of her father in her, with his untamable kink to her hair and crooked teeth she couldn't afford to fix.

Adrienne undid her seat belt and stepped into the aisle to trade seats. She didn't mind the window, and to be honest, she should have a good view of New York City as it slipped away with her dreams.

"My name is Cynthia Dempsey," the woman said as she sat down.

Adrienne was surprised, figuring the woman would dismiss her once she'd gotten her way. Slipping her book into the seat-back pocket, she returned the smile, hoping the woman didn't notice her crooked teeth the way she'd noticed her perfect ones. "Adrienne Lockhart."

"That is a great name. It would look fantastic on a billboard in Times Square."

Or on a fashion label. "I'm not meant for the spotlight, but thank you."

Cynthia settled in, fidgeting with a large diamond engagement ring on her finger as they started to pull away from the concourse. Her fingers were so thin, and the band too large, that the massive jewel seemed to overwhelm her.

"Are you getting married soon?"

"Yes," Cynthia said, sighing, but her face didn't light up the way it should. She leaned in more like she was sharing gossip, as though her wedding would be the talk of the town. "I'm marrying William Taylor the Third at the Plaza next May. His family owns the *Daily Observer*."

That said it all. It *would* be the talk of the town. Adrienne was sitting three inches from the woman, but it might as well have been miles. She would probably spend more on her wedding than Adrienne had inherited when her father died. "Who's doing your dress?" The only common ground they could share was fashion, so Adrienne steered the conversation that direction.

"Badgley Mischka."

"I love their work. I actually interned with them for a summer in college, but I prefer daily wear that appeals to the modern working woman. Sportswear. Separates."

"Are you in the fashion industry?"

Adrienne winced. "I was. I had a small boutique in SoHo for a few years, but I had to close it recently."

"Where would I have seen your work?"

Turning in her seat, she gestured to the gray-and-pink blouse she was wearing. It had an unusual angled collar and stitching details that made it distinctively hers. "Since I'm out of business, this is your last chance to see an Adrienne Lockhart design."

"That's a shame." Cynthia frowned. "I love that top, and my friends would, too. I guess we just don't make it downtown often enough."

Three years Adrienne had worked, struggling to get her pieces out there. Sending samples to stylists in the hopes that something would make it into a magazine. Wearing her clothes out at every opportunity to catch the eye of someone with influence. It was just her luck that she would meet that person on the plane home.

"Ladies and gentlemen, we are next for takeoff. Flight attendants, please prepare for departure and cross-check."

Adrienne sat back and closed her eyes as the plane taxied. She hated to fly. Hated turbulence. Hated the feeling in her stomach when she took off and landed. She went through a reassurance ritual each time, telling herself cabs were much more dangerous, but it didn't help.

The engines roared loudly as the plane started speeding down the runway. Adrienne opened her eyes for just a second and saw Cynthia nervously spinning her engagement ring again. She didn't seem to like flying either. That made Adrienne feel a little better about her own fears.

The wheels lifted off, the plane shuddering as the air current surged them upward. The slight shake was enough for Cynthia's elbow to slip from the armrest, sending her ring flying. It fell to the floor between their feet, disappearing several rows behind them as the plane tipped into the air.

"Oh, hell," Cynthia complained, looking around her.

This was the absolute worst time for it to happen. Adrienne was about to say something reassuring when a loud boom sent all thoughts of missing rings from her mind. The plane shook violently and pitched downward. Adrienne looked frantically out the window. They weren't that far off the ground yet.

She clutched the arms of her seat and closed her eyes, ignoring the groans of the equipment and the screams of the people around her. The pilot came on to announce an emergency landing, the edge of nerves in his voice. It made Adrienne wish she'd paid more attention to the safety briefing instead of talking to Cynthia. Networking with dead people was pointless.

Doing what she could remember, Adrienne leaned forward, rested her head between her knees and wrapped her arms around her legs. Her eyes squeezed tightly shut as another loud boom sounded, the lights went out in the cabin and the plane lurched.

There was nothing left to do but pray.

One

Four weeks later

"Cynthia?"

The voice cut through the fog, rousing her from the grips of the protective sleep her body insisted on. She wanted to tell the voice to go away, that she was happier asleep and oblivious to the pain, but it insisted she wake up.

"Cynthia, Will is here."

There was something nagging at her brain, a niggling sensation that made her frown with confusion every time someone said her name. It was like a butterfly that would sit on her shoulder for a moment, then flitter away before she could catch it.

"Maybe I should come by later. She needs her rest." The man's deep voice pulled her closer to consciousness, her body responding to him against its will. Since she'd first heard it, he'd had that power over her.

"No, she's just napping. They want her up and moving around, engaged in conversations."

"What's the point? She doesn't know who any of us are."

"They said her memory could come back at any time." The woman's voice sounded a touch distraught at his blunt observation. "Talking to her is the best thing we can do to help. I know it's difficult, but we all have to try. Cynthia, dear, please wake up."

Her eyes fluttered open as she reached the surface of consciousness. It took a moment for everything to come into focus. First there were the overhead hospital lights, then the face of the older woman that hovered above her. Who was she again? She dug through the murky recesses of her brain for the answer. They told her she was her mother, Pauline Dempsey. It was discouraging when even the woman that gave her life barely registered in her brain.

That said, she looked lovely today. Her dark hair was nicely styled. She must've been to the salon, because the strands of gray were gone and it swung lightly, as though it had been trimmed. She had a silk scarf tied around her neck with flowers that matched the blue in her pants suit and the green in her eyes. Wanting to reach up and adjust the scarf, she was thwarted by the sling protecting her broken arm. Just the slightest change would've made it much more flattering and modern, although she didn't know why she thought so. Amnesia was a strange companion.

"Will is here, dear."

The worry slipped from her mind as Pauline pressed the button to raise the head of the hospital bed. Self-consciously, she smoothed her hair and tucked it behind her ears, readjusting her sling to make her heavy, casted arm more comfortable.

Sitting up, she was able to see Will seated at the foot of her bed. They said he was her fiancé. Looking at the handsome, well-dressed man beside her, she found that very hard to believe. His light brown hair was short but long enough on the top for him to run his fingers through it. His features were aristocratic and angular, except for the full lips she found herself watching while he talked. His eyes were blue, but she didn't know exactly what shade because she avoided looking him in the eye for long. It was uncomfortable, and she wasn't sure why. Maybe it was the lack of emotion in them. Or the way he scrutinized her with his gaze.

She knew absolutely nothing at all, didn't even know what she didn't know, but she had managed in the past few weeks to realize that her fiancé didn't seem to like her at all. He always lingered in the background, watching her with a furrowed brow. When he didn't appear suspicious or confused by the things she said or did, he seemed indifferent to her and her condition. The thought was enough to make her want to cry, but she didn't dare. The moment she got agitated, nurses would run in and give her something to numb everything, including her heart.

Instead she focused on his clothes. She found she enjoyed looking at everyone's different outfits and how they put them together. He was in his usual suit. Today it was a dark, charcoal gray with a blue dress shirt and diamond-patterned tie. He ran a newspaper and could only visit during lunch break or right after work, unless he had meetings. And he had a lot of meetings.

That or he just didn't care to visit her and it was a convenient excuse.

"Hello, Will," she managed, although it didn't come out quite the way she wanted. The multiple surgeries they'd done on her face went well, but there was more healing still to go. The accident had knocked out all her front teeth. They'd implanted new ones, but they felt alien in her mouth. Even after all the stitches were removed and the swelling had gone down, she had a hard time talking with the large, white veneers. And when she did say anything, she sounded like she'd swallowed a frog from the smoke and heat that had seared her throat.

"I'll leave you two alone," Pauline said. "Would you like some coffee from the cafeteria, Will?"

"No, I'm fine, thank you."

Her mother slipped out the door, leaving them in the large, private hospital room reserved for VIP patients. Apparently she was a VIP, because her family had made a large donation to the hospital several years back. At least that's what she was told.

"How are you feeling today, Cynthia?"

Realizing she wasn't sure, she stopped to take a personal inventory. Her face still ached and her arm throbbed, but overall she didn't feel too bad. Not nearly in as much pain as when she'd first woken up. If they'd told her she'd been locked inside a giant dryer, tumbling around for three days, she'd have believed them. Every inch of her body, from the roots of her hair to her toenails, had ached. She could barely talk or see because her face was swollen so badly. She'd come a long way in the past few weeks. "Pretty good today, thank you. How are you?"

Will frowned slightly at her but quickly wiped the expression away. "I'm well. Busy, as usual."

"You look tired." And he did. She didn't know what he looked like normally, but she'd noticed that the dark smudges and lines around his eyes had deepened each time she saw him. "Are you sleeping well?"

He paused for a moment, then shrugged. "I guess not. It's been a stressful month."

"You need some of this," she said, tugging on the tube that led to her IV. "You'll sleep like a baby for sixteen hours, whether you want to or not."

Will smiled and it pleased her. She wasn't sure if she'd seen him smile since she came to, but it was enough of a tease that now she wanted to hear him laugh. She wondered if he had a deep, throaty laugh. The suited man looking at her oozed a confidence and sexuality that even a sterile hospital couldn't dampen. Certainly his laugh would be as sexy as he was.

"I bet." He glanced down, looking slightly uncomfortable.

She never knew what to say to him. She was constantly being visited by friends and family, all of whom she'd swear she'd never seen in her whole life, but none of those chats were as awkward as talking to Will. She'd hoped it would get easier, but it just didn't. The nicer she was to him, the more resistant he seemed, almost like he didn't expect her to be civil.

"I have something for you."

She perked up in her bed, his sudden announcement unexpected. "Really?"

Her room had been flooded with gifts early on. It seemed like every flower and balloon in Manhattan had found its way to Cynthia's hospital room. Since then, the occasional arrangement came in from family or even strangers who heard about her story on the news. Being one of three survivors of a plane crash was quite newsworthy.

Will reached into his pocket and pulled out a small velvet box. "The airline called earlier this week. They've been sifting through the wreckage, trying to identify what they can, and they found this. They traced the laser-etched serial number on the diamond back to me."

He opened up the box to reveal an enormous diamond ring. Part of her wanted to believe it was a well-made costume piece, but after what she'd seen of her family and their large, plentiful and authentic jewelry, she knew it was breathtakingly real.

"It's beautiful."

Will frowned. Apparently that was the wrong response. "It's your engagement ring."

She almost laughed, but then she noticed the serious look

on his face. Owning a ring like that seemed preposterous. "Mine?" She watched as Will gently slipped the ring onto her left ring finger. It was a little snug, but with that arm broken and surgically pinned, her fingers were swollen. She looked down to admire the ring and was pleased to find there was a vague familiarity about it. "I do feel like I've seen this ring before," she said. The doctors had encouraged her to speak up anytime something resonated with her.

"That's good. It's one of a kind, so if it feels familiar, you've seen it before. I took it to be cleaned, had the setting checked to make sure nothing was loose, but I wanted to bring it back to you today. I'm not surprised you lost it in the accident. All that dieting for the wedding had made it too loose."

"And now it's too small and I look like I'm the loser of a boxing match," she said with a pout that sent a dull pain across her cheek. It didn't hurt as much as her pride. She had no idea what her wedding dress looked like, but she was certain that if she'd thought she looked better in it thin, the swelling wouldn't help.

"Don't worry, there's still plenty of time. It's only October. May is a long way off, and you'll be fully recovered by then."

"May at the Plaza." She wasn't sure why, but she knew that much.

"It's slowly coming back," he said with a smile that didn't quite go to his eyes. Standing, he slipped the ring box back into his pocket. "I'm having dinner with Alex tonight, so I'd better get going."

She remembered Alex from his visit the week before. He was Will's friend from school and quite the flirt. Even looking like she did, he told her she was beautiful and how he'd steal her away if she wasn't Will's fiancée. It was crap, but she appreciated the effort. "You two have fun. I believe we're having rubber chicken and rice tonight."

At that, Will chuckled. "I'll see you tomorrow." He reached out to pat her hand reassuringly.

The moment he touched her, she felt a familiar shiver run down her spine. Every single overworked nerve ending in her body lit up with awareness instead of pain. Her chest tightened, her hand involuntarily gripping his to maintain the connection it craved.

His touches, however brief or fleeting, were better than any morphine drip. Just the brush of his fingers against her skin made her feel alive and tingly in a way totally inappropriate for someone in her present condition. It had been that way since the first time he'd pressed a soft kiss against the back of her hand. She might not know him by sight, but her body certainly recognized her lover. The pleasurable current cut through everything—the pain, the medication, the confusion.

If only she reacted that way to a man who liked her. The thought was like a pin that popped the momentary bubble that protected her from everything else in her life that was going wrong.

Will looked at his hand, then at her with a curiosity that made her wonder if he were feeling the same thing. She noticed then that his eyes were a light blue-gray. They were soft and welcoming for a moment, an inner heat thawing his indifference, and then a beep from the phone at his hip distracted him and he pulled away. With every inch that grew between them, the ache of emptiness in her gut grew stronger.

"Good night, Cynthia," he said, slipping through the door.

With him gone, the suite once again became as cold and sterile as any other hospital room and she felt more alone than ever.

Alex sat sipping his drink on the other side of the table. He'd been quiet through the first two courses. Will always appreciated his friend's ability to enjoy silence and not force a conversation to fill space. He understood that Will had a lot on his mind, and letting him get through a glass of Scotch would make the discussion easier.

He'd asked Alex to join him for dinner because he needed to talk to someone who would be honest. Most people just told him what he wanted to hear. Alex was one of the few people he knew with more money than he had and who wasn't inclined to blow smoke up his ass. He was a notorious playboy and typically not the first person Will went to for romantic advice, but he knew Alex wouldn't pull any punches when he asked for his opinion on what he should do about Cynthia.

What a mess their relationship had become. To think that a few short weeks ago, he didn't believe it could get any worse. It was like daring God to strike him...

"So, how's Cynthia faring?" Alex finally asked once their entrées arrived, forcing Will out of his own head.

"Better. She's healing up nicely but still doesn't remember anything."

"Including the fight?"

"Especially the fight." Will sighed.

Before Cynthia had left for Chicago, Will had confronted her with evidence of an affair and broke off the engagement. She'd insisted they could talk things through once she got back, but he wasn't interested. He was done with her. He'd been on the phone with his real estate agent when the call came in that Cynthia's plane had crashed. When she woke up with no memory, he wasn't sure what to do. Continuing with his plan to leave seemed cruel at that point. He needed to see her through her recovery, but he would leave as planned when she was back on her feet.

At least that was the original idea. Since then...the situation had gotten confusing. This was why Alex was here. He could help him sort things out before he made it worse.

"Have you told her yet? Or should I say *again?*"

"No, I haven't. I think once she's discharged, we'll talk.

We're rarely alone at the hospital, and I don't want her parents getting involved."

"I take it she isn't back to being the frigid shrew we all know and love?"

Will shook his head. Part of him wished she was. Then he could walk away without a pang of guilt after her recovery. But she was an entirely different woman since the accident. He'd had a hard time adjusting to the changes in her, always waiting for Cynthia to start barking orders or criticize the hospital staff. But she never did. He made a point of visiting her every day, but despite how hard he fought it, Will found he enjoyed the visits more and more. "It's like she's been abducted by aliens and replaced with a pod person."

"I have to admit she was quite pleasant when I came by the other day." Alex put a bit of filet mignon in his mouth.

"Yeah, I know. Every time I visit her, I just sit back and watch in disbelief as she asks people how they are and thanks everyone for visiting or bringing her things. She's sweet, thoughtful, funny…and absolutely nothing like the woman who left for Chicago."

Alex leaned in, his brow furrowed. "You're smiling when you talk about her. Things really have changed. You *like* her," he accused.

"What is this, prep school again? Yes, she is a more pleasant person and I enjoy being around her in a way I never have before. But the doctors say her amnesia is probably temporary. In the blink of an eye, she could be back to normal. I refuse to get reinvested only to end up where I started."

"*Probably temporary* can mean *possibly permanent*. Maybe she'll stay this way."

"Doesn't matter," Will said with a shake of his head. It was just like Alex to encourage him to make a risky move. "She may not remember what she did, but I do. I can never trust her again, and that means we're through."

"Or this could be your second chance. If she really is a different person, treat her like one. Don't hold a past she doesn't even remember against her. You could miss out on something great."

His friend turned his attention back to his steak, leaving Will alone with his thoughts. Alex said the words he'd been afraid to let himself even think. Being with Cynthia was like meeting a woman for the first time. He found himself rushing from the office to visit her or thinking about how she was while he needed to concentrate on the front page flash for the *Observer*. And today…he'd felt an undeniable sizzle of awareness when they'd touched. He'd never had that intense a reaction to her before. He didn't know if it was the fright of nearly losing her for good or her personality change, but there was a part of him that wanted to take Alex's advice.

Of course, Alex didn't keep a woman long enough for the relationship to sour. It might not seem like it now, but the old Cynthia was still lurking inside her. That woman was miserable and unfaithful and stomped on his feelings with her expensive stiletto heels. Will had broken it off with her, and he had no doubt she'd be back before long. He wasn't going to lose his heart, freedom or any more years of his life to this relationship.

The doctors said she could probably go home soon. He was certain Pauline and George would want her back at their estate, but Will was going to insist she return to their penthouse so he could care for her. Having her at home was the natural choice. It was closer to the doctor, and being around her own things would be good for her.

And if it jogged her memory and she went back to normal? It would save him the trouble of breaking up with her a second time.

"Would you like to trade seats?"
The words floated in her brain, her dreams mixing reality

and fantasy with a dash of pain medication to really confuse things.

"My name is Cynthia Dempsey."

The words made her frown even in her sleep. Cynthia Dempsey. She wished they would stop calling her that. But she also didn't know what she'd rather have people call her. If she wasn't Cynthia Dempsey, shouldn't she know who she really was?

And she did. The name was on the tip of her tongue.

The boom of an engine bursting into flames dashed the name from her mind. Then there was only the horrible, sickening feeling of falling from the sky.

"No!"

She shot up in bed, hurting about a half dozen parts of her body in the process. Her heart was racing, her breath quick in her throat. The nearby bed monitor started beeping, and before she could gather her composure, one of the night shift nurses came in.

"How are we, Miss Dempsey?"

"Stop calling me that," she snapped, the confusion of sleep removing the buffer that edited what she shouldn't say.

"Okay…*Cynthia*. Are you all right?"

She saw it was her favorite nurse, Gwen, when she reached over and turned on the small light above her bed. Gwen was a tiny Southern girl with naturally curly ash-blond hair and a positive but no-nonsense attitude about life. She could also draw blood without pain, so that instantly put her at the top of Cynthia's list.

"Yes." She wiped her sleepy eyes with her good hand. "I just had a bad dream. I'm sorry for snarling at you like that."

"Don't you worry your pretty li'l head about it," Gwen said, her thick Tennessee accent curling her words. She turned off the alarm and checked her IV fluids. "A lot of trauma patients have nightmares. Do you want something to help you sleep?"

"No, I'm tired of…not feeling like myself. Although I'm beginning to wonder if that has anything to do with the medication."

Gwen sat at the edge of the bed and patted her knee. "You had some pretty severe head trauma, honey. It's possible you might never feel exactly like you used to. Or that you won't know when you do. Just make the most of how and what you feel like, now."

Cynthia decided to take advantage of the only person she could really talk to about this. Will wouldn't understand. It would just upset Pauline. Her mother spent every afternoon with her at the hospital, showing her pictures, telling stories and trying to unlock her memory. Saying she didn't feel like herself would just be an insult to Pauline's hard work.

"It feels all wrong. The people. The way they treat me. I mean, look at this." She slipped her arm out of the sling and extended her pale pink cast to show off her engagement ring.

"That's lovely," Gwen said politely, although her dark brown eyes had grown twice their size upon seeing the massive diamond.

"Don't. We both know this could feed a third-world country for a year."

"Probably," she conceded.

"This doesn't feel like me. I don't feel like some snobby uptown girl that went to private school and got everything she ever wanted. I feel like a fish out of water, and I shouldn't. If this is my life, why do I feel so out of touch with it? How can I be who I am when I don't know who I was?"

"Honey, this is a little deep for a three o'clock in the morning conversation. But here's some unsolicited advice from a Tennessee fish in Manhattan waters. I'd stop worrying about who you were and just be yourself. You'll go crazy trying to figure out what you should do and how you should act."

"How do I do that?"

"For a start, stop fighting it. When you walk out of this

room to start your new life, embrace being Cynthia Dempsey. Then, just do what you feel. If the new Cynthia would rather go to a Knicks game than the symphony, that's okay. If you've lost your taste for caviar and expensive wine, eat a cheeseburger and drink a beer. Only you know who you want to be now. Don't let anyone change that."

"Thank you, Gwen." She leaned forward and embraced the nurse who felt like her only real friend in her new life. "I'm being discharged tomorrow. Will is taking me back to our apartment. I have no idea what's in store for me there, but when I'm in the mood for burgers and beer, can I call you?"

Gwen smiled wide. "Absolutely." She wrote her cell phone number in the small notebook Cynthia had been using to keep notes. "And don't worry," she added. "I can't imagine any future with Will Taylor in it being bad."

Cynthia nodded and returned her reassuring grin. She just hoped Gwen was right.

Two

Will watched Cynthia walk through their apartment as if she were taking a tour of the Met. He had to admit the place felt like a museum sometimes with all the glass, marble and leather. It wasn't what he would've chosen, but everything served its designated function, so he didn't really care.

She examined each room, admiring the artwork, running her fingers over the fabrics and seeming visibly pleased with what she saw. She should like it, he mused. She and her god-awful decorator picked it all out.

Cynthia moved slowly, the stiffness of her muscles slowing her down. The doctors had changed the cast on her arm to a brace so she could remove it to shower for the last few weeks until it was fully healed. All the bandages and stitches were gone now and only the faintest of discoloration was visible on her face and body. If not for the slight limp and the brace, you might never know what kind of trauma she'd undergone.

Pauline had a hairstylist come to the hospital to do her hair before she was discharged. The hospital staff had to trim a good bit of the length off as it was singed from the fire, but the stylist turned their chop work into a chic, straight style that fell right at her shoulders. It was an attractive change, and he found himself admiring it as the town car brought them home. Her face looked so much better, and the hairstyle accented it nicely. A new style for the new woman in his life.

There was a thought that would bring him nothing but trouble.

Will turned and found Cynthia staring at the large engagement portrait they had hanging in the living room. *Damn.* He'd gone through the apartment and put away all her pictures as Pauline had asked, but he had to miss the giant one on the wall. As far as he knew, she hadn't seen any pictures of herself from before the accident. But now that she had, he expected her to have Dr. Takashi on the phone in an instant, threatening him with malpractice. Personally, he thought the doctor had done a great job even if she didn't look exactly the same.

But nothing happened. She stood silently studying it for a moment, and then she continued to the back of the apartment. The chime of his phone distracted him with an email from work, and he heard her shout from down the hall as he read it.

"This bathroom is huge! Is this mine?"

"Does it have a sunken whirlpool tub?"

"No."

"Then no," he said with a chuckle. "That's just the guest bath. Ours is off the master bedroom." And not three weeks before the crash, she'd complained that their bathroom was too small. He'd asked if she was throwing a cocktail party in there, and she'd scowled.

Clipping his phone to his belt, Will followed her to see if she'd gotten lost somewhere. He found her standing in her closet, her eyes glazed over at the selection in front of her.

After a moment, she reached out and started flipping through the neatly hung outfits.

"Dior. Donna Karan. Kate Spade. Are these…mine?"

"Every bit. You moved my stuff out of the closet six months ago to make room for your ever-expanding shoe collection."

At that, she turned to face the wall of shoes behind her as though she hadn't noticed it before. She whipped open a box of Christian Louboutins and stepped out of the loafers she'd worn home. The black patent-leather pump with the red sole slipped on without hesitation. "They're a little too big," she said.

That was odd. "Well, if your feet shrunk in the accident somehow, I'm sure you'll have fun replacing all of these with your new size."

She shot him a look of pure disbelief as she slid on the other shoe. She was a little unsteady on the five-inch heels at first, reaching out with her good arm to brace herself, then a wide grin spread across her face. Maybe now the bedazzled leather contraptions would be appreciated.

"I'm sure an insert would do the trick. I wouldn't dare waste all these." She turned back to the clothes, flipping through a few dresses he remembered her wearing at one society event or another. "Why is it that I recognize all these designers and understand their importance, but my own mother is a stranger?"

That was a good question. He had no idea how amnesia worked. Will ran his fingers through his hair and shook his head. "Maybe your brain just remembers what was most important to you."

Cynthia stopped in that moment and turned to him. The look of wonder faded from her face. "Did I really prefer shoes over my own family?"

Will shrugged. "I don't know. I'm not the person you confided in."

She slipped out of the shoes, placed them gently into their box and returned them to the shelf. No longer seeming to enjoy her closet, Cynthia brushed past Will on her way into the bedroom and disappeared down the hall.

He followed her out and found her sitting on the couch, staring blankly at the hideous modern art piece hanging over the dining-room table. "Are you all right?"

She nodded stiffly, but he didn't believe her. "I feel like everyone is tiptoeing around me. That there's an elephant in the room that everyone can see but me. If I ask you some questions, would you answer them for me? Honestly?"

He frowned but agreed before sitting on the couch beside her. They needed to talk, and there was no sense in putting it off.

"Are you and I in love?"

She certainly didn't hold back, so he opted to do the same. "No." Candy-coating the truth wouldn't help. She needed to know.

"Then why are we engaged?" Her wide green eyes looked a touch disillusioned.

"We're not."

"But…" Cynthia started, looking down at her ring.

"We were in love a long time ago," Will explained. "Our families were old friends, and we dated through college. I proposed two years ago, and then you changed and we grew apart. Your family doesn't know yet, but I broke off our engagement right before you left for your trip."

"Why?"

"You were having an affair. The benefits of staying with you were outweighed by the betrayal."

"Benefits? That sounds like an awfully cold way to talk about it."

"It's the truth. We didn't have a relationship left, really. Your father and I were collaborating on a project that would've been extremely lucrative for both our companies.

Your father prefers to work with family, so I was trying to see it through, hoping we'd weather the rough patch. When I found out you'd been having an affair for quite some time, there was no choice left. Even if the project fell through, the wedding was off. I told you I'd be out of here by the end of October. Plans obviously changed after the accident."

"You're staying?" She looked up at him with hopeful eyes that gripped at his heart. Somehow it seemed wrong to punish her for what felt like someone else's sins.

"No. I'll be here until you're well. Then we will announce the breakup and I'll move out as planned."

Cynthia nodded in understanding, but he thought he saw the shimmer of tears in her eyes before she looked away. "I must've been a horrible person. Was I always that way? You couldn't have loved me if I was."

"I liked the woman you were when we met. I wasn't fond of the woman you became after college."

She swallowed hard and looked down at the hands she had folded in her lap. She said she wanted the truth and she was getting it, even if it was hard to hear. "Was I nice to anyone?"

"Your friends and family, for the most part. You spoiled your little sister. But you had a short fuse if someone upset you."

"Am I anything like that now?" she asked.

"No," he said. "You're quite different since the accident."

"But...?"

"But, I wonder how long it will last. The doctor says the memory loss is temporary and anything could trigger it all to come back. At any moment, the woman sitting in front of me could disappear."

"And you don't want that to happen, do you?"

The face of his fiancée, so familiar, yet so different, looked at him. Her green eyes were pleading with him, and he noticed golden flecks in them he'd never seen before. It was beautiful the way the colors swirled together, pulling him in.

It made him want to keep looking, to find details he'd missed before. How long had he been with Cynthia but never really knew her? It made him wonder if he ever actually loved her or just the idea of them together. The smartest, most beautiful girl at Yale and the captain of the polo team. Both from wealthy families that ran in the Manhattan society circles. It was a match made in heaven.

But this was completely different. He wanted to know the woman sitting beside him. He wanted to help her explore the world and learn who she was and who she wanted to be. And he shouldn't. He should tell her it didn't matter if she got her memory back. But that wasn't true, and she asked for honesty. "No, I don't want that."

"You know," she said thoughtfully, "there's a part of me missing, and that bothers me. But from what I've heard, I think maybe it's better this way. Better if I don't remember and just start fresh."

Her words resonated with him. Alex had said this could be a second chance for their relationship. But could he offer it? This woman had betrayed him, abused his trust and threw away what they had together. Did the fact that she didn't remember doing any of it make a difference? He wasn't sure. "You always have a choice."

Cynthia's brow furrowed, a line deepening between her eyebrows in concern. Her last dose of Botox must've worn off during her hospital stay. It was refreshing to see her express real emotions, even if it cost her a few wrinkles over time. "What do you mean?" she asked.

"At any moment your memory could come back. When that happens, you always have the choice of continuing to be the person you want to be instead of going back to your old ways. You can make a fresh start."

She nodded, continuing to watch her hands and seemingly building up the courage to ask more questions. "I know you didn't like me, but were you at least physically attracted to me before the accident?"

"You were a beautiful woman."

"You're dodging the question," she said, her gaze meeting his. Her irritation brought a red blush to her cheeks that chased away some of the yellow discoloration from her bruises. She was so full of emotion now. Her skin flushed with anger and embarrassment, her eyes teared up with confusion and sadness. It was such a welcome change from the ice princess he knew.

It made him wonder what she would be like to make love to. Will's groin tightened, and he pushed the thought out of his mind. He was leaving, and he'd never find out the answer to that question, so it was better he didn't think about it. "I'm not. You were beautiful. Every guy at Yale wanted you, including me."

"That picture in the hall…"

"Our engagement portrait?"

"Yes. I don't look much like that now. I doubt I ever will again." There was another new expression on her face, a vulnerability that Will wasn't certain he'd ever seen before. Cynthia was many things, but she rarely showed weakness. The woman sitting beside him had a fragility about her that made him want to comfort her. He'd never felt that urge before. And he certainly shouldn't feel that way about Cynthia, of all people.

Unable to fight the need, he reached out and ran a thumb over her cheek. The swelling was almost entirely gone now. "Before, you were like a statue in a museum. Perfect, but cold." The tips of his fingers tingled as they glided over her soft, ivory skin. "I think flaws give character, and you're much prettier now. On the inside, too."

Cynthia brought her hand up to cover his where it rested on her cheek. "Thank you for saying that, even if it isn't true." Wrapping her fingers around his hand, she pulled it down into her lap, where she held it tightly. "I don't know everything I did to you, but I can only imagine. I'm sorry. Do you think you could ever forgive me for the things I did in the past?"

Tears gathered in Cynthia's eyes, and it made his chest ache to see her upset. The way she clutched his hand was like a silent plea. The guilt of crimes she couldn't remember was eating her up. She wasn't asking him to love her again. Or to stay. Just to forgive her.

Seeing her like this, spending time with her the past few weeks, had roused new and different feelings for her. Feelings that if left unchecked could lead him to getting hurt again. He couldn't allow that, even if every part of his body urged him to take the chance. But maybe he could offer her absolution. And then, in time, perhaps more.

"Maybe what we both need is a clean slate. To put everything behind us and start over."

Cynthia's eyes widened in surprise. "Start over?"

"Yes. Both of us just need to let go of the past and move forward. You can stop worrying about what you've done and who you were and just focus on what you want for your future. And maybe I can stop punishing us both for things we can't change."

"What does that mean for you and me?"

That was a good question. One he wasn't really ready to answer, but he'd do the best he could. "It means we start over, too. We're strangers, really. We have no reason to trust each other, much less love one another. What, if anything, happens between us will take time to determine."

"And what about this?" Cynthia held up her hand, her large engagement ring on display.

"Keep wearing it for now. This is our business. We don't need anyone offering their two cents, especially our families. This is a decision we have to make ourselves."

Forgiving her was the right thing to do. Cynthia nodded,

a faint smile curving the corners of her full, pouty lips. Her eyes were devoid of tears now and lit with the optimistic excitement of new opportunities. After weeks of seeing her so battered and beaten down, she was almost glowing. She did truly look beautiful, regardless of what she thought. So beautiful that he was filled with the undeniable urge to kiss the smile from her lips.

He leaned in, pressing his mouth gently against hers. It was little more than a flutter or brush across her abused skin. A silent reassurance that things would be okay even if it didn't work out between them.

At least that was the idea. In an instant, his whole body responded to the touch of her, and he knew the reaction at the hospital had not been a fluke. He'd felt a surge there but had convinced himself he'd just gone too long without sex. Maybe that was still the case, but every nerve ending urged him to cup her face and drink her in. But he didn't dare. For one thing, he didn't want to risk hurting her, since she wasn't fully healed. And for another, it was the first step down a rabbit hole he'd be unable to crawl back out of.

"Think about what you want your life to be. And what you want us to be," he whispered against her mouth. Then he pulled away before he changed his mind and did something he'd regret.

Cynthia didn't feel beautiful. She didn't care what Will said. That kiss was likely just out of pity. To make her feel better for realizing she'd been a miserable, beautiful woman once and a sweet, broken woman now. She could tell he was uncomfortable about it. His cell phone rang, and he immediately took the opportunity to disappear into what she supposed was his home office. She was left to her own devices to make herself comfortable and get used to her new, old home.

The problem was that it didn't feel much like home. The whole space had an institutional quality about it. She appreciated the clean lines and indulgent fabrics, but it was too modern for her taste. There wasn't a single piece of furniture that called to her to come and snuggle into it. The couch was firm, cold leather. The chairs were wood or metal without much padding. After poking around, she settled into the bedroom to watch television. The large, luxurious bed was perfectly comfy and the ideal place to lose herself in some mindless entertainment.

When that lost its appeal, she decided to take advantage of her bathroom and take her first real shower since the accident. She undressed and gently removed her arm brace, making a face when she saw how skinny and pale her arm was underneath. Then she stood languishing under the multiple streams of boiling hot water for a good half hour. The shower made her feel more human, more normal, but once she sat down at her vanity, normal disappeared.

They'd kept mirrors from her the first few weeks. Pauline—er…*her mother*—had insisted on it. She didn't want Cynthia to get upset. Cynthia didn't know how she was supposed to look, but it didn't take a mirror to realize there had been a drastic change, and not for the better. The pained expressions on the faces of those who knew her were enough. So she hadn't asked for a mirror.

Then one day Dr. Takashi removed the last of the bandages and brought a hand mirror with him. Cynthia hadn't wanted to look at first. She had no idea what she would find. Her mother was an attractive older woman, and her younger sister, Emma, was cute in an awkward, teenaged way, but she had no assurance she didn't take after her father. George was a regal, commanding man, but she wouldn't say he was handsome. He had a nose like a hawk's beak and eyes that appeared cold and beady when he focused unhappily on hospital staff.

Looking in the mirror that first time had been hard, but it had gotten easier. Every time she saw her reflection she looked better. The expressions on her family's faces were encouraging. But the one thing no one had done was bring her a photo of how she looked before the accident. Her mother had brought in a shoebox of pictures, pointing out different people for her to try to remember, but not a single one had her in it.

Returning to the apartment, one of the first things she was greeted with was a large canvas photo of her and Will. She was almost startled when she rounded the corner to the living room and came face-to-face with her former self.

It looked like the kind of engagement portrait that would go in a newspaper announcement. Her long, dark hair was swept over her shoulder, revealing large sapphire earrings that complemented the royal blue dress she had on. Will was looking handsome, yet casual, in khakis and a light blue dress shirt. They were sitting together under a tree.

The woman in the portrait had elegant, delicate features. Her skin was flawless and creamy, her eyes a clear, bright green. Her makeup was applied so well it took a keen eye to notice she had any on at all. She looked every bit the daughter and fiancée of two powerful Manhattan families.

She'd expected to be upset when she finally saw a photo of herself, but she found the experience to be oddly vacant. It was like looking at a picture of a stranger. Disconnected.

Now, watching her reflection in the partially foggy mirror, it was hard not to draw the comparison and catalog the vast differences. The high cheekbones and delicate nose had taken the brunt of the accident. Time would tell if the plates and implants Dr. Takashi used would bring back the prominent features.

Only the eyes and the smile looked like the portrait to her. Smiling in the mirror, she admired her new teeth. They were much like the photo, though they, more than anything, still felt wrong when she tried to eat or talk. And the eyes…well, the expression behind them was different. Perhaps when the photo was taken she wasn't so confused.

Her hairstylist had blown her hair straight after cutting it that morning. It was twisted up in a towel at the moment, but she knew the unruly kink would be back once it dried. She wondered how she would blow it out again with one good arm, then decided she didn't care enough to bother. Wavy hair was the least of her worries.

With a sigh, Cynthia poured a bit of lotion from the hospital into her hand and gently rubbed it into her face and neck. It was supposed to help with the scars and overall healing. Somehow, she doubted it would do enough.

More than anything, even if she never looked like she did in that portrait again, Cynthia wanted to feel right in her own skin. And she just didn't. Lotion couldn't fix that.

"I bet that felt nice after all those sponge baths."

Cynthia snapped her head to the side and found Will leaning casually against the doorframe, his hands buried in his pockets. He'd been working for so long she'd forgotten he was home.

Self-consciously, she tugged her towel up higher over her breasts and held it tight to keep it from coming undone. She could admit to herself she was attracted to him—the blush spreading across her face was evidence of that—but being mostly naked in front of him was a distinct disadvantage. They may very well have seen each other naked a hundred times, but she had no recollection of it. He was a stranger, like he'd said earlier. Everyone was, including herself.

He noted her reaction, stiffening instantly and taking a step back. "I'm sorry. This probably makes you uncomfortable. I didn't think about that. I'll go."

"No, don't," she said, reaching out to him before she could stop herself. She didn't want to be alone any longer. She'd wandered, confused and sad, through the apartment all afternoon, hoping anything would jog her memory. Having him here, even with her half-naked, was a welcome change.

He paused, then held up a finger. "I'll be right back."

Will returned a moment later with a fluffy, ice-blue chenille bathrobe. "This was your favorite. You liked to wear it in the evenings to curl up on the couch and read a book with your favorite glass of wine."

Cynthia stood, still clutching her towel, and let him drape the robe over her shoulders. She slipped into the enveloping warmth, dropped the towel to her feet and tied the robe closed. It immediately quelled her concerns, covering her from neck to toe.

With the hot shower and the soft robe, she really couldn't imagine feeling any better. At least until her fingers brushed his as she adjusted the collar. The glide of his skin across hers sent a tingle down her spine that had nothing to do with the cool marble and tile bathroom. She gasped softly and his fingers pulled away. She turned to look at him, her heart beating erratically in her chest. How did he do that to her with a simple touch? "This is great," she muttered sheepishly. "Thanks."

He nodded, stepping back, but still watching her in a way that made her want to readjust her robe under his scrutiny. She wished she understood what was behind his gaze. He had an intensity about him that attracted her, but she couldn't decipher what it meant when he focused it on her. Was it desire? Subdued anger? Curiosity?

"Are you hungry?"

Apparently, she was confusing the look of lust with hunger. "Yes," she admitted. The last thing she remembered eating was some manifestation of Salisbury steak before she was discharged.

"What would you like?"

"Anything but hospital food," she said with a smile.

"Okay," he said, matching her grin. "I'll go pick up something and bring it back. There's a nice Thai place not too far from here. Would you like to try that?"

"Sure. Just don't get me anything too spicy," she offered. She had no idea if she would like it or not, but that should be safe enough.

With a nod, Will turned and left. Seconds later she heard the front door open and close behind him.

To prepare for dinner, she detangled her hair and went to the closet in search of something comfortable. Some of the clothes were too tight, but Will mentioned she'd been dieting for the wedding. She flipped farther into the racks, finding some older things in a larger size. She was eyeing a stretchy pair of yoga pants when the phone rang.

For a moment, she was startled, not quite sure what to do. It felt like answering someone else's phone, but it wasn't. The call might very well be for her. Telling herself that it could be Will, she went into the bedroom and picked the phone up off the receiver. "Hello?"

"Cynthia?" the man's voice asked, but it wasn't Will. This voice was deeper, quieter, as though he didn't want anyone to hear him but her.

"Yes, this is Cynthia. Who's calling?"

The man hesitated for a moment. "Baby, it's Nigel."

Nigel. The name didn't ring even the slightest bell, although he said it as if it explained everything. But he called her "baby." She didn't like that at all. "I'm sorry, I don't remember you. I've had an accident and the doctors diagnosed me with amnesia."

"Amnesia? My God, Cynthia. I've got to see you. These past few weeks I've been going mad with worry. Your cell phone is disconnected. I couldn't get into the hospital because I wasn't family. All I know is what I read in the papers about the crash, and it wasn't much. Please tell me I can see you soon. Maybe tomorrow while Will is at work?"

Cynthia's stomach sank. Will hadn't elaborated on the details of her affair, but it didn't take much to realize Nigel was her lover.

Will's voice crept into her mind. *You have a choice.*

And she did. The past was the past. Will had offered her a clean slate and with it, perhaps a future together. At first, she hadn't been quite certain what to make of it. She had obviously been unhappy with Will before and wasn't certain if a bump to the head could make everything better between them. But she at least wanted to try. For now, she wanted Will to stay. The man on the phone would ruin any chance they had.

"No, I'm sorry."

"Baby, wait. I'll take an early train from the Bronx and meet you for coffee."

"No. Please stop calling. Goodbye." She disconnected and set the phone back onto the cradle. A few seconds later it rang again, the same number lighting up the screen. She didn't answer it. The phone finally went silent and she waited nervously for a moment, but he didn't call back.

That done, she took a deep breath and returned to the closet to get ready for her first dinner with Will.

Three

William sat at his desk, staring blankly at his laptop. After dinner, he'd returned to his office to work as he usually did. He spent most evenings working. Newspapers didn't run themselves, and given that most of his days were filled with unproductive but necessary meetings, it was the only time he could dig through his email and actually get something done. Some people might've been bothered by the long hours he put in to keep the *Observer* at the top of its game, but Will didn't mind. In fact, over the past few years, his office and unending stream of work had become a sanctuary from his failing relationship.

And yet tonight, with at least a hundred unread emails in his inbox, he couldn't focus on the work. His thoughts kept straying to Cynthia.

He watched her roam around the apartment through the glass French doors that separated his office from the living room. When he'd left to pick up dinner, he thought things were okay between them. Better than okay if he let himself think too long about her shower-damp skin and the skimpy bath towel she was wrapped in. He hadn't seen that much of Cynthia's body in quite some time, and his visceral reaction to her was immediate and powerful. Fortunately the brisk walk to the takeout place had served as a cold shower, and by the time he had returned, he had it under control.

But now she seemed nervous around him. They'd eaten their Thai food in the dining room, filling the space between bites with harmless small talk. But he noticed an edge that wasn't there earlier. When the phone rang, she nearly launched from her seat to beat him to answering it, and it was just Pauline checking to make sure she was settled in. The mother and daughter chatted while he cleaned up dinner and disappeared into his office.

Will couldn't help but think that maybe she'd picked up on his attraction and it made her uncomfortable. He'd mentioned the possibility of a future together—nothing was impossible—but he wasn't sold on the idea. He just wished his body and brain were on the same page.

He wasn't surprised when she disappeared into the bedroom fairly early. She was probably exhausted after her first day out of the hospital. On top of the physical challenges, their talk had stirred up a lot of information that could be stressful to process. Dumping their past on her today was probably a mistake with her fragile condition, but she wanted honesty.

Given her nerves around him, he should probably sleep in the guest room tonight. It would make everyone more comfortable, and he could use the space to keep objective about all this.

With the apartment silent and dark, Will was able to focus on his work again. He finally shut down for the night near midnight. He would be up the next day by six, but those were standard hours for him. He could sleep when he was dead. Or retired. Whichever came first.

The next morning, he was up, dressed and having coffee by the time Cynthia stumbled into the kitchen. She was wearing navy silk pajamas under her robe, her hair pulled into a ponytail. Her eyes were still blurry and her face lined from a night of heavy sleep. The woman he knew would never let anyone, not even him, see her like this. She always emerged from the bedroom with her hair and makeup done. Will had to swallow his surprise in a large swig of coffee. He really needed to come to terms with Cynthia as a new person, but it was hard to change his every expectation of her.

"Good morning," she said, gently rubbing her eyes.

"Morning," he replied, getting up to refill his mug. "Would you like some coffee?"

"No," she said, wrinkling her nose. "I tried some in the hospital and didn't like it."

Will returned to the table and slid a plate with a couple pieces of buttered whole-wheat toast toward her. He couldn't stomach much more than that this early, but if he didn't eat something, he'd never make it through the morning column reviews. "I made some toast. There's tea and cocoa in the cabinet if you're interested."

Cynthia settled into one of the kitchen chairs and took a piece of toast from the plate. She seemed a lot more relaxed than she had last night, and Will was relieved. Perhaps some time alone in the apartment would help her adjust.

"I hate to leave so soon after you got up, but I need to get to the office. I'm going to try not to stay too late."

"You work a lot," she commented.

Will shrugged, rising from the table and putting his mug in the sink. "I do what I have to. Now, the maid should be here today around noon, so you won't be alone. I asked her to make dinner so we don't have to go out. She's planning to go through all the classic recipes so you can try them. I think we're up for pot roast tonight."

"Okay." She nodded, although her brow was wrinkled in confusion again.

"What's wrong?" he asked.

"It feels weird to have someone cook and clean up after me. I guess it probably shouldn't, but it does."

"I'm sure you'll adjust to the luxury of it in no time, especially once you try Anita's eggplant parmesan. She's truly gifted in the kitchen. If you need anything," he said as he slipped into his suit coat, "call my cell phone. I've left you a list of numbers on the refrigerator, including your folks and some friends if you get lonely."

"Thank you," she said, standing up to see him out.

They walked to the front door, where he grabbed his laptop bag. "I'll see you tonight." On reflex, he started to lean in to give her a goodbye kiss. In that fraction of a second, he noticed her eyes widen and her body tense up. Given her reaction after yesterday's kiss, it was probably a horrible idea, even as a casual goodbye. He stopped short, pulling back awkwardly, and instead threw up a hand to wave and darted out into the hallway.

Traveling down the elevator, Will could only shake his head. What the hell was he doing? He certainly wasn't acting like a man on the verge of moving out. He was getting sucked in by her, like quicksand. The more he struggled, the more he was sure to sink.

It was better he get to the office as quickly as he could. At least there, he knew what he was doing.

Cynthia stared at the closed apartment door, more confused than ever. Her heart had fluttered in her chest when she thought he might kiss her. Their kiss the night before hadn't really counted and just left her anxious for more. Will had set his hostility aside after their talk yesterday, but things were hardly on track for serious romance. She knew it was too soon for any of that. Kisses would only complicate things.

But that didn't stop her from fantasizing about what his kisses would feel like or how his mouth would taste. When he leaned close to her, the scent of his spicy cologne was enough to send her pulse racing. It made her thankful she wasn't still hooked up to hospital monitors that might give away her attraction to him.

Shaking her head, she locked the door and went back to her room to get dressed for the day. She wasn't exactly sure why—she had no intention of leaving—but it seemed like the thing to do. Reaching into the back of the closet, she pulled out a pair of khaki pants and a long-sleeved blouse in a dusty shade of pink and then slipped them both on with a pair of loafers.

Returning to the kitchen, she boiled water for tea and slathered another piece of toast with raspberry jam she found in the refrigerator. When the tea was ready, she poured a cup, grabbed her toast and went to explore the room Will had said was her private office.

She'd glanced at it briefly the day before but hadn't ventured inside. After their talk—and Nigel's call—she was afraid of what she'd find. Today, she wanted to tackle her past head-on and set it aside for good. She settled at the glass-and-chrome desk and ate while taking it all in. A large space on the desk was cleared off for her laptop, which had been destroyed in the crash. Stacked around it were glossy magazines and file folders. It was all very neat and precise. It made her want to reach out and shuffle some of the pages around. There was simply too much perfection.

Across from her desk were a red leather love seat and a chrome-and-glass coffee table. Several large advertising posters and a few framed magazine ads were hung on the wall for products she recognized. Her best guess was that these were campaigns she designed. Her family told her she was a successful partner in a Madison Avenue advertising agency.

Looking at them, a feeling of unease washed over her.

Not only were they completely unfamiliar, but she had no thoughts about the marketing strategies that went into them. All she could come up with was that she liked the dress one of the models was wearing. That was it.

Without her memory, she was going to need a career backup plan, and fast. Especially if Will opted to leave as planned. He'd left the door open for a relationship, putting the ball in her court to decide what she wanted. If she'd really hurt him as badly as he'd said, he was right to leave and she wouldn't blame him. But last night's discussion with Nigel had shown her that she did want to try for more with Will. She wanted him to stay, and not just for the financial support.

And yet, knowing he always had one foot out the door made her hesitant to invest too much. She might be the one to get hurt this time. It was a sobering thought that sent her scrambling for a chore to occupy her mind.

Cynthia opted to start shuffling through paperwork, partially out of curiosity and partially out of the hope that it might jog something in her head. She opened files and thumbed through pages about different campaigns and clients. Mostly it was unfamiliar gobbledy-gook. The advertising lingo was completely lost on her.

Setting them aside, she opened a drawer in her desk and fished around. At the front of the drawer were neatly stacked and aligned office supplies. Further back was a pile of envelopes. Cynthia pulled them out and eyed the outside. They were all addressed to her. Some of the postmarks went back as much as a year.

Picking the oldest one, she removed the letter and started reading it. It was a love letter from Nigel. An actual, handwritten love letter. It was sort of an odd thing to do in this day and age, but he explained in the first one how he thought it was the only sincere way to express how he felt. Email was cold and impersonal. She'd probably kept the incriminating letters for their sentimental value.

With a sigh, Cynthia sat back into her chair. She knew she'd had an affair, but being confronted with evidence of it was disconcerting. It was quite the romance they'd shared. He was a struggling artist she met at a gallery show. Since that time, they'd been meeting secretly at lunch, going away for weekends together under the guise of business trips and taking advantage of Will's long hours by flaunting their relationship in the apartment she shared with him.

The letters were more romantic than she'd expected from a fling. She couldn't know what she wrote back to him, but they seemed to be in love. It boggled her mind, not jiving with what everyone told her about herself. How did an uptown society girl fall in love with a poor artist from the Bronx? She didn't understand. Was she just using Nigel, or was she too embarrassed to be with him publicly? Daddy and Mother certainly wouldn't approve. Did loving Nigel and marrying Will somehow give her the best of both worlds?

Cynthia felt sick and was thankful to only have toast in her stomach. She thought she wanted to regain insight into her old life, but now she never wanted to remember the truth. She wanted to erase it all.

Piling the letters into a heap on her desk, she dug around for anything else incriminating. Her laptop and cell phone were gone, so any digital evidence of her relationship with Nigel went down with the plane. If and when she got a new computer, she'd purge anything left behind in her accounts. Will had already mentioned replacing her cell phone. She'd make sure to ask for a new number that Nigel couldn't get his hands on. In her office file cabinet, she found a folder with various cards from Valentine's Day and her birthday inside. None were from Will. Those were added to the pile, as were some photos of Cynthia and a blond man she didn't recognize. They looked far too cozy and the location far too tropical. She could take no chances with this. It all had to go.

By the time the housekeeper, Anita, arrived, Cynthia had

a fairly large stack of things to destroy. She went out to meet the woman in the living room. She was a pleasantly plump older woman with graying hair. Quite efficient, she'd already begun dusting the mantle over the fireplace when Cynthia found her there.

The fireplace. Perfect.

"Miss Dempsey." She smiled, although Cynthia didn't detect much sincere warmth behind it. "It's so good to see you back home. I'll do my best to stay out of your way."

Her housekeeper didn't seem to like her either. Did anyone? "Please, call me Cynthia. And you're no trouble. I'm happy to have someone here with me. Let me know if I can help you with anything. I feel bad just sitting around watching you work."

Anita looked as though she were struggling to hide the surprise on her face, simply nodding when she apparently failed. "Thank you, Miss Dempsey, but I can manage. Do you need anything before I get started?"

Since she asked… "Actually, I'm a little chilled this afternoon. I'd love to just curl up with a book in here. Any chance we could get the fireplace going?"

That Saturday was an unseasonably warm fall day. By this time in November, people were usually heavily bundled or shoveling out of the first snow, but it was in the high sixties. Will had started off that morning working in his office as usual, but seeing Cynthia wander aimlessly through the apartment tugged at him with guilt.

He'd made a habit of focusing on work to avoid dealing with her before the accident, but he didn't need to work this much. And for the first time in a long time, he didn't want to. He wanted to spend more time with Cynthia. Which is why he deliberately stayed in his office this long—the pull she had on him was too strong. But he couldn't stay in there forever.

Shutting his laptop down, he came out of the office and found her reading on the couch. She had a paperback romance in her hands. It hadn't come from any of the bookshelves in the house. "What are you reading?"

"A book I bought on the corner yesterday. I'm really enjoying it."

Will nodded, trying not to let his surprise show, because it just worried Cynthia when she realized she was doing something out of character. Honestly, the less she realized was different, the better. This Cynthia was all wrong, but all right by him.

"I noticed you had the fireplace going the other day, but it's fairly warm out today. Would you be interested in getting out of the apartment? Maybe take a walk around the park?"

The grin that met his question made him feel even guiltier for waiting this long. Her face lit up like a child in front of an ice cream sundae. She put her book down, carefully marking the page. "Should I change?"

Will hadn't really noticed what she had on before that. If he had, he might've had another surprise to hide from her. She wore a pair of tight, dark denim jeans, gray ankle boots and a soft gray sweater that went down past her hips. She'd put a hot-pink belt over it and some chunky pink bracelets to match on her good arm.

"Wow, pink," he commented.

She smiled and ran her hand over the belt. "I've decided pink is my favorite color. Do you like it?"

He knew the only reason Cynthia had that belt was for a retro eighties-style charity fundraiser they'd attended last year. She appeared quite taken with the splash of color now. Cynthia seemed to get a lot of enjoyment from putting an outfit together. It was a fun look for her. Her hair was down and slightly curly. Her face was fresh and free of makeup. She really looked lovely.

For a walk in the park, her outfit suited just as well as his khakis and polo shirt. "You look fine. Will you be okay to walk in those boots?"

She stood, feeling around in them for a moment. "I think so. They're pretty comfortable, and I think my daily strolls are paying off."

Will grabbed a light windbreaker from the closet and ushered Cynthia out ahead of him. They took the elevator to the ground floor of their building, waving to the doorman as he greeted them by name and held the large golden door open for them.

It didn't take them long to reach Central Park. They walked silently down the sidewalk, crossing over into the forest of reds, oranges and golds that autumn had ushered in. It had always been his favorite time of year. Fall in Manhattan was the best. The cooler temperatures, the changing leaves, the Thanksgiving parade…it just gave him a sense of inner peace no other time of year provided, like the world was slowing down in preparation for winter.

"I love the fall," Cynthia said, happily stomping on crisp leaves under her boots. "I think it might be my favorite time of year. Of course, I don't remember much about the other three seasons, so I'm withholding judgment for now."

Will smiled, reaching to his hip for the phone that had chirped several times since they left the apartment. He thumbed through the messages but didn't get very far before he felt Cynthia's insistent tug on his arm. He looked up to see her pointing at one of the city's million hot-dog carts.

"Let's find out if I like hot dogs."

Will slipped the phone back into its holster and followed her over to the cart. Something as simple as a hot-dog vendor had filled her with excitement. It was so contagious that he was eager to have one, too, and he hadn't bothered to in years.

They stopped at the cart and ordered two hot dogs and sodas—his piled on with sauerkraut and mustard, hers with ketchup, mustard and sweet relish. They found a bench and sat down with their lunch.

He'd polished off about half of his when he looked over and noticed Cynthia's hot dog was completely gone. She dabbed the corner of her mouth to remove some rogue mustard, still chewing the last bite. Apparently she did like hot dogs. "Would you like another one?"

"No," she said, shaking her head and sipping her soda. "That was just enough. There are a million things out there for me to try. I'll gain ten pounds if I overdo it. It's just one of many things I have to figure out."

Will watched her expression grow somber. She sipped her drink thoughtfully and watched a leaf blow by. He popped the last of his hot dog into his mouth, chewing and swallowing before he spoke again. "What are you thinking about?"

Cynthia sighed and sat back against the bench. "I'm thinking of what a mess I'm in. In a few weeks' time, you could be gone. I don't think I can go back to my old job if my memory doesn't return. I have no real skills I remember. I didn't even know if I liked hot dogs until a few minutes ago. What am I supposed to do?"

He'd considered this subject as he'd watched her lie in that hospital bed for weeks. She was fortunate that her income wasn't important. Anyone else might be crippled by it. "Well, you may not know it, but you do have a healthy trust fund and stock portfolio. You could live comfortably on that for quite some time."

"I'll go stir crazy in that apartment doing nothing. Especially if I'm there alone."

Will noted the way she looked at him when she said the last part. She didn't want him to leave. And sitting here with her in this moment, he didn't want to leave either. She needed to feel secure in her situation. At least then he would know she wanted him to stay for the right reasons. "I've also spoken to your boss, Ed. He understands the circumstances, and if and when you're ready to come back, okay. But if not…you could always try working for your dad."

"And do what? I don't understand any of that technical stuff. I don't want to get paid to sit at a desk at Dempsey Corp. playing solitaire just because I'm the boss's daughter."

He had to admire that. Working for her father or sitting around the house would've been the easy thing to do, but she wanted more. "You have the luxury of trying something new. You've got a world of opportunities ahead of you. What would you like to do? Anything interest you?"

She thought for a moment before she answered. "Clothes. Clothes are all that has really caught my attention. Not just buying and wearing them, but putting pieces together. Admiring the lines of a blazer or the texture of a fabric. I'm not quite sure what to do with it, though."

Will had noticed the last few weeks in the hospital how she had mentioned people's clothing, complimenting them, asking about fabrics and where they bought one piece or another. It seemed to be a natural interest for her. "Would you like to try designing clothes? Or maybe be a stylist for fashion shoots or something?"

Cynthia turned to him, her green eyes wide. "Is designing clothes really an option? I watched a lot of reruns of some fashion reality show in the hospital, and it looked interesting. I may not be any good at it, though."

"Doesn't mean it would hurt to try. We'll get you some sketch paper and colored pencils. See what you come up with. You don't have to be the next Versace, but you can play around and have some fun with it."

She broke into a wide smile and flung her arms around his neck. He was taken aback by her enthusiastic embrace, but he didn't pull away. He wanted to encourage this new side of her, even if he wouldn't be around to see it come to fruition.

Instead, he wrapped his arms around her and pulled her close. She buried her face in his neck and he breathed in the

scent of her—a mix of a floral shampoo, a touch of perfume
and the warmth of her skin. He recognized her favorite fragrance, yet it was different somehow. Something underlying
it all was new and extremely appealing. His body noted the
difference and responded to it despite his brain's reluctance.
His pulse quickened and his groin stirred in an instant.

He had tried to wish away his attraction to her, and yet
Alex's words taunted him. This could be their second chance.
He'd offered them both a clean slate, and the only thing keeping him from taking this opportunity was his own stubborn
sense of self-preservation. Yes, the woman he proposed to
had abused everything he gave her. But this was an entirely
different woman despite their resemblance. No matter how
hard he fought it, she intrigued and aroused him like no
woman had before.

What would it hurt to see where this could go, even if
only to soothe his own curiosity? He could certainly keep
his heart out of the situation to avoid disaster. If things went
awry or she regained her memory, he could easily walk away,
no harm done. And if he could keep their relationship going
long enough to satisfy George Dempsey, it would boost his
business. It seemed like a win-win situation if he could let
himself give in to it.

Cynthia pulled away slightly, stopping to look up at him.
She was clearly excited by her new design adventure, but
her expression shifted as she gazed into his eyes. Something
changed in that moment, and he could feel the difference, too.
The attraction she felt for him was just as strong. He could
tell by the way her breath caught, her lips parting slightly and
tempting him closer.

She wanted him to kiss her. And he wanted to. He wanted
to know how she would touch him. What sounds she would
make. How she would feel in his arms. Letting his body and
his curiosity win over, he leaned in and captured her lips
with his own. There was an immediate connection when he

touched her. This wasn't just a test. It was a real kiss, unlike what they'd shared before. A thrill raced through his body, a tingling in the base of his spine urging him to pull her closer. The need built quickly inside, pushing him to take more from her.

Cynthia leaned into him and placed one hand gently on his cheek. His tongue brushed hers, the taste and feel of her new and unexpected, like silk and honey. The hand resting on her hip slid upwards, caressing her side and tugging her to him. She whimpered quietly against his mouth, a soft, feminine sound that roused a primal reaction in him. He'd never been this turned on by a kiss in his life.

Everything about her, from the gentle caress of her hands to the flutter of her eyelashes against his cheek, started his blood boiling. There was an innocence, a sweetness. She had no agenda, no motives for offering herself to him. She just gave in to her desires and urged him to do the same. It took everything he had not to scoop her off the bench, carry her back to the apartment and claim her as his own.

Unfortunately, by the time he carried her four blocks to their apartment, he would realize it was a mistake. Pulling away, he stayed close, their breath warm on each other's skin. They sat still for a moment, his mind whirling with the implications of what he'd just done. He needed to keep his brain in charge instead of his crotch, or he'd make a mess of everything.

The loud melody of his phone broke the trance. The gap between them widened, Cynthia self-consciously straightening her clothes while he checked the caller ID. Apologizing, he took the call, ending the conversation as quickly as he could. "Let's go get you those art supplies," he suggested, when no other words seemed appropriate.

They gathered up their hot dog wrappers and soda cans, tossing them into a nearby garbage receptacle, and headed back out of the park and toward the nearest craft store.

This time, as they traveled, he felt Cynthia's fingers tentatively seek out his own. He couldn't remember holding hands with a girl since high school, and it was charming and unexpected. Hesitating for only a moment, he captured her small hand and they walked together out of the park.

With every step, he felt himself being pulled further in by the fascinating woman he refused to love.

Four

"I'm so glad you called me, Cynthia. I was wondering how you were adjusting to real life."

Cynthia smiled across the table at her former nurse, Gwen. She was glad to have someone to talk to. Anita the housekeeper seemed concerned every time she tried to strike up a conversation, and when she spoke to her family, they'd start on her again about coming to stay with them. Even her sister, Emma, had dropped hints, probably at their mother's urging. She enjoyed the time she'd spent with Pauline—they'd even had brunch on Sunday—but there were expectations there that she didn't know how to fill. Gwen was the only person Cynthia knew from after the accident, and she appreciated having someone around who didn't look at her as if she were possessed.

"It's been interesting. Fortunately, I've managed to avoid a lot of people. I guess since I was in such bad shape, they want to wait as long as possible to see me. I don't think it will last much longer. My mother is planning a big, fancy party to celebrate my recovery. I tried to block most of it out yesterday when she mentioned mailing invitations and hiring an orchestra to play. It sounds over the top and absolutely miserable."

Gwen smiled and squirted some ketchup on her cheeseburger. "The people in your life care about you, as weird as all of this is for everyone involved. The sooner the new you gets out there, the sooner everyone will adjust. Are you planning on returning to work?"

"I don't think so."

"Sometimes getting back in an old routine can help."

"Maybe, but I think it's an impossibility. I mean, if I were a doctor, would you want me to jump back in the saddle and operate on you, hoping my years of medical training would magically come back to me?"

Gwen wrinkled her nose. "I guess not."

"I was in advertising, which I know isn't like brain surgery, but I remember nothing about it. I don't really have an interest in it either."

"So what are you going to do? Become one of those society wives that organize fundraisers?"

"Uh, no," she groaned. "Right now I'm just trying something out."

"Do tell," Gwen urged, taking a large bite.

Cynthia thought about the pages and pages of clothing designs she'd sketched over the weekend. At first, it had been a wreck. At least twenty sheets of paper had been crumpled into balls and tossed in the trash bin. But then they started getting better. She let go of her inhibitions and the ideas started flowing. The color combinations she put together worked even when she worried they wouldn't. The pieces coordinated beautifully. She was itching to see some of them leap off the page and onto a hanger. But that was a whole other hurdle to climb over. She might be a good artist and a horrible seamstress.

"I'm trying my hand at designing clothes. Just sketches right now, but I did what you told me and I'm following my instincts. Trying to do what my heart tells me feels right."

"Fashion design? Wow. Are you enjoying it?"

She couldn't hide her smile. "I am. I just sketch and sketch and when Will comes looking for me, I'm shocked to find I spent hours working on it."

"Sounds like you may be on to something."

"I think so. I mean, right now it's just sketches, but I'm thinking about getting a sewing machine and trying to actually make some of it."

"You should open a boutique and show at Fashion Week," Gwen encouraged.

Cynthia had to laugh at her friend's enthusiasm. "You are way ahead of me on this. First thing I have to do is figure out how to thread a bobbin. Then, if what I make doesn't suck, I'll go from there. I'm a long way from Bryant Park."

"But it's progress in the right direction. You're building your new life. I think that's great."

That made her feel good. She had Will's support, but a part of her wondered if he felt obligated to be her cheerleader. Her mother had feigned interest at brunch, but Cynthia could tell she'd been hoping her daughter would settle for being a society housewife like she was or at least go work for the family company. Knowing Gwen supported the choice made all the difference. "It is. I just wish everything else was working out, as well."

"Like what?" Gwen asked with a concerned frown.

"Like Will and me." Cynthia sighed, the weight of her situation heavy on her shoulders. He was sending conflicting signals. One minute he's discussing how she can support herself after he moves out and the next they're kissing on a park bench and holding hands. But even then, there was a part of him holding back. He was determined to keep one foot firmly out the door for a quick escape. That wasn't a good sign. "I don't know where I stand with him. With us. He seems distant sometimes."

Cynthia knew she couldn't tell anyone, not even Gwen, that they'd called off the engagement. Or about Nigel. He'd started calling again after Will left in the mornings. She'd considered telling Will, but it just seemed like dragging up the past after they had agreed to set it aside. Eventually he would stop calling. He had to.

"Maybe he's just not sure how to deal with the changes. You guys have been together a long time. It's like being with a new person. Whether the changes are good or bad, it's still an adjustment."

She looked down at her half-eaten burger and fries, which she was pleased to discover she adored, and nodded. Gwen was right. This had to be just as hard on Will as it was on her. Even as they kissed in the park, she could sense an internal battle raging inside him. The part that wanted her and the part that held back for whatever reason had fought hard. She wasn't certain which side won. They'd held hands in the park on the way home, but he holed up in his office after that.

"Has anything happened between the two of you since you went home?"

"Just a kiss," she said, the memory of it flushing her cheeks like a schoolgirl. Given her amnesia, it was like having her first kiss all over again.

"A kiss is something. If he didn't like you, I doubt he'd bother kissing you."

"But nothing has happened since then."

Gwen took a sip of her drink and shrugged. "I wouldn't worry about that. He might be concerned about your recovery. Or preoccupied with his company. But let me ask you a question. Do you *want* something to happen?"

Cynthia frowned. "What do you mean?"

"I mean, you've sort of inherited Will by default. Yes, you were technically with him for years, chose to be with him, but to the new you, he's a stranger. What if you just ran into Will on the street? Would you be attracted to him?"

Cynthia tried to imagine crossing paths with Will in an alternate universe where they'd never met. Perhaps she dropped something and he stopped to pick it up for her. The Will in her mind smiled and she found herself immediately drawn into the blue-gray eyes that watched her. The powerful aura that surrounded him was hard to resist, even in her fantasy. His strong build, his confident stride, the way he moved so gracefully yet with commanding purpose.

A pool of longing settled low in her belly and made her squirm uncomfortably in her seat. It was just like the memory of their kiss. Yes, she was attracted to Will. She couldn't remember their past, but her taste in men had certainly not changed since the accident, even if everything else had.

The question was whether she could allow herself to fall for him. He'd told her to think about it. And she had. She wanted to give them a second chance, but she didn't trust herself. She had no idea what she was capable of. She didn't want to hurt Will again. Letting this relationship and its baggage go might be better for everyone concerned. But it was difficult to ignore a man like Will.

"I think under any circumstances he'd be pretty hard to resist," she conceded.

"Then why are you fighting it? The hard work is done. You've already landed one of the most eligible men in Manhattan. Regardless of the past, I see no reason why you shouldn't allow yourself to indulge in this relationship."

Cynthia could think of a dozen reasons why she shouldn't be with Will and only one reason why she should. Unfortunately, that one reason had the tendency to trump all her good sense.

She wanted him. Badly.

And whether she should or not, she was going to try her damnedest to build a new relationship and keep him.

* * *

George Dempsey sat across from Will, the large mahogany conference-room table scattered with paperwork. The lawyers had prepared everything they needed for the product collaboration on the e-reader; the finer details just needed to get ironed out.

Unfortunately, Will could tell they wouldn't get very far today. His almost-father-in-law had more pressing issues on his mind.

"I'm worried about Cynthia," he said, staring blankly at a contract.

"The doctors say she's healing well."

"I'm not worried about her face," George grumbled, tossing down the page. "I'm worried about her head. Pauline tells me she's not going back to the ad agency, but she still refuses to work for me."

"I don't think she's passionate about electronics like you are. She never has been. Why would that change now?"

"Maybe because everything else has. She's doodling dresses all day. I feel like I don't even know my own daughter anymore."

"That's only fair. She doesn't know you, either."

George's brow furrowed in irritation. "Don't make light of this. I'm worried about her emotional health. And, frankly, I'm worried about this wedding."

Alarm bells suddenly sounded in Will's head. As far as he knew, no one but Cynthia and Alex knew about their breakup. They were toying with the idea of trying again, but nothing was set in stone. Their kiss in the park had been everything he imagined it would be and more, but it worried him. They had the potential of moving too quickly, crashing and burning before the ink on the e-reader deal had dried. He'd taken a step back and tried to distance himself the past few days. He ordered her a present to be delivered to the apartment and hoped to take her out to dinner tonight, but he couldn't predict the future. The paperwork on the table didn't mean a damn if George thought the relationship was in jeopardy. "She's been through a lot. A May wedding might be too soon. She could need more time to adjust."

George leaned across the table and speared Will with his steely gaze. "What about you? Are you getting cold feet?"

Will shouldn't have been surprised by the older man's blunt nature, but it always caught him off guard. "Why would you say that?"

"You two haven't been the lovebirds you once were. Back in school you couldn't keep your hands off each other. Even before the crash I sensed a distance. I don't want to believe you're a big enough bastard to leave her after her accident, but people shock me every day."

"I have no intention of leaving Cynthia in her condition. No one can guarantee what happens after that. Any relationship can fail at any time, even when you're trying."

George cocked a curious eyebrow up at Will. "You know I prefer doing business with family. They won't stab you in the back to please stockholders. If you have any reservations, you'd damn well better tell me before I sign off on this." George slid some papers across the table.

"Mr. Dempsey, this e-reader collaboration is smart business. It benefits both our companies. The *Observer* is a family company as well. We've got sixty years invested in its success. I understand your reservations, but know that with or without this marriage, we're fully behind the success of Dempsey Corp."

The old eagle eyed him, reading the sincerity Will hoped was etched into his face. He seemed satisfied for now. "You better be. But one other thing, Taylor."

Will hesitated to ask. "Yes?"

"I know a lot of people in this town. Business aside, if you hurt my little girl, I'll do everything in my power to crush you and this newspaper like a bug."

Will swallowed the lump in his throat and nodded. And to think, he'd only been worried that Cynthia might hurt him.

When Cynthia arrived back at the apartment from her lunch with Gwen, the doorman waved her over to the desk. "Miss Dempsey?"

Surprised, she went to the counter. "Afternoon, Calvin. How are you today?"

Calvin smiled and she noted the sincerity that hadn't been there the first time she'd met him. "Doing fine, Miss Dempsey. I have a delivery for you. It's fairly heavy. Would you like me to have it brought up?"

"That would be wonderful, thank you."

She continued on to the apartment, and within minutes there was a ring at the door. She opened it up to find one of the other building attendants, Ronald, carrying a large white box. "Oh, my goodness," she said, stepping out of the way. "Just set it over on the table."

Digging in her wallet past her newly reissued credit cards and ID, she took some money out for Ronald and thanked him as he quickly exited.

Alone, she returned to the box. The delivery slip was addressed to her. She couldn't imagine what it could be. She took a pair of scissors from the drawer near the entryway and sliced open the tape.

Inside was a big, beautiful, expensive, top-of-the-line sewing machine. She couldn't even lift it out of the box and had to settle for admiring it from the top. It was shiny white with chrome accents. Stuck down along the side of the foam packaging, she found the owner's manual. Since she had a while before Will would come home and help her unpack the sewing machine, she opted to study the instructions in preparation for its first use.

Around the time she finished reading, she heard Will at the door. Leaping from the couch, she rounded the corner to meet him just as he stepped inside. He looked at the expression on her face and then turned to the kitchen, where the large box was still sitting.

"I see it arrived."

"It did!" she exclaimed. "Did you buy it for me? It's wonderful."

"I ordered it this morning. They assured me it was the best you could buy and that they'd deliver it today."

Without hesitation, she put her arms around him, hugging him tightly and kissing him. Her intent had been to say thank-you, but once her lips met his, her plans unraveled. Will snaked his arms around her waist, pulling her tight against him. He had been distant since their last kiss and she'd thought maybe he wasn't interested, but there were no doubts once his tongue slid across hers and his fingers pressed hungrily into her flesh.

It felt so good in his arms. So...*right*...unlike everything else in her life. Most days, she felt like a body snatcher, wearing Cynthia Dempsey and her life like a skin. Nothing felt real or normal except sketching clothes and being with Will. Certainly taking another chance with Will was the right choice.

Pulling back at last, she said, "Thank you." She just knew her face was turning beet-red from being pressed so firmly against the full length of his body. It made her feel self-conscious.

Will didn't seem to notice. "You're welcome," he said with a devious smile. "If I'd known you'd react like this, I would've bought it two years ago. Or at least last week."

Cynthia smiled awkwardly at his statement, still wrapped tightly in his arms. She wasn't sure if she wanted him to let go or to pull her closer and kiss her again. "I...I've been reading up on how to use it," she stuttered.

He held on for a moment longer before releasing her to take a few steps back. "Already studying?"

The short distance was enough to clear her head and return her focus to the topic at hand. "Yes, I think I could have it up and running by tomorrow morning. Do you think we could take a little field trip tonight? I'd love to get some supplies to play with. Fabric, thread, maybe some buttons?"

Will let his computer bag drop to the floor and shuffled out of his jacket. "We can. I was actually thinking I would take you out for dinner tonight anyway. We can go by the fabric store on the way. Just let me change out of this suit."

Cynthia prepared quickly, knowing most fabric stores would be closing soon. He changed and they grabbed a taxi to whisk them to the Garment District. They took the old-fashioned elevator up to Mood, and she entered it like she would a sacred cathedral. Will loitered near the entrance doing business on his phone while she disappeared into the three stories of fabrics.

Triumphant, she greeted him a half hour later with a large black Mood bag filled with everything she might need. The dress form that wouldn't fit in the sack would be delivered tomorrow. One of the employees had helped her, making sure she had all the basics, and gave her a good idea of what to do with them.

It was all very exciting. She had this surge of energy she hadn't had since the accident. It was like the world had opened up to new possibilities. Fate had closed the door on her past, but as the operator slid open the metal grate of the elevator door, it was like he was opening a window to her exhilarating new future.

"Did you buy out the store?" Will asked, pushing open the downstairs door as she breezed past him.

"Not today. Maybe next week."

"It's good to have goals," he said with a laugh. "Are you ready for dinner?"

"Yes," she said. Lunch had worn off long ago, but she'd been too wrapped up in her new sewing machine to notice.

"There's a steakhouse a few blocks east of here that I've been wanting to try. Does that sound okay?"

"Sounds great."

Will took her bag and carried it for her as they made their way to the restaurant. As they stepped inside, Cynthia immediately felt underdressed and stopped dead in her tracks. The dark restaurant had paneled walls and deep burgundy tablecloths, delicately folded napkins and enough flatware to confuse an etiquette expert. Her slacks and sweater just didn't seem up to par. Will had to nudge her forward so the door could close behind them.

"This place is too nice," she whispered.

"You're fine," he assured, pushing her toward the maître d's desk. "Two, please."

Cynthia followed the two men through the restaurant to their table. They were seated at a secluded two-top in a corner where they wouldn't be disturbed by other diners. The waiter was obviously under the impression that they were on a date. It certainly didn't feel like one. At least not with Will eyeballing his cell phone again instead of his menu.

"Would you like to try one of our fine wine selections this evening?" the waiter asked when he arrived.

Will put his phone aside and looked expectantly to her, but she didn't know what to say. He'd mentioned before that she liked to drink wine, but she was really just craving a tall, cold glass of Diet Coke. So she said so.

Will nodded. "A Diet Coke for the lady and a merlot for me, please."

Once the server was gone, Cynthia tried to focus on the menu. There were so many things she hadn't tried yet, but there'd been almost nothing she hadn't liked. Except brussel sprouts. She had to remember to tell Anita that before she made them again. Tonight, however, she decided on a surf and turf to sample a few new items at once.

When the ordering was done and they were left alone with

their drinks, Cynthia noticed for the first time how romantic the restaurant was, especially their quiet little alcove. A large stone hearth contained a fire that roared on one wall, the warm lighting casting everything in a golden glow. She hoped it would do wonders for her skin tone, which still wasn't quite back to the perfect cream it once was. It certainly looked good on Will. The flickering of the fire sent shadows across the angular planes of his face and darkened his hair to a deep mahogany color. The flames reflected in his eyes as he watched her intently from across the table.

She drew in a ragged breath, her tongue darting across her lips to moisten them. His gaze dipped down to her lips for a moment and back to her eyes with a small smile. The heat of his stare made her intensely aware of her whole body. And his. The button-down shirt he'd changed into was dark green. It strained across his chest and shoulders, the hard muscles underneath fighting to be free of the restraint. Being pressed against him earlier had set her imagination wild. She wanted to know how those bare muscles would twitch under her hands. Or how the wall of his chest would feel when her breasts flattened hard against him.

"This place is very nice," she said, reaching for her soda and taking a large sip to moisten her suddenly dry throat.

"It is," he agreed, sitting back in his chair. "I'm glad we decided to try it."

"How was work?" Cynthia desperately sought out a topic of conversation that wouldn't make her think of touching Will and fisted her hands under the table to keep from reaching out to him.

"Busy, as usual. I saw your father today."

That would definitely cool her ardor. "Yes, Mother mentioned he was going to see you. How is he?"

"Good. We were going over the finer details of our product collaboration. It should be ready to launch in the spring."

"What are you two doing, exactly?"

"We're working on e-reader technology. His people have managed to create a touch screen so light, thin and cheap that before long, everyone will have one. We're hoping to even give them away with long-term e-subscriptions to the paper."

"Is your paper having trouble?"

"No, we're still performing well, but a lot of other papers aren't. It's all about the internet these days. I added online subscriptions a few years back, but I think e-readers are really the next big thing in the publishing industry. I want the *Observer* and Dempsey Corp. at the front of the surge. To take my company to the next level as a top-tier performer. It's what I've fought for years to do."

Cynthia nodded, although she had no real idea what it was all about. She loved the feel of a book in her hand, and it would take time before she would be willing to give that up to a gadget. But it sounded promising for the two companies. A big boost in the industry. Maybe if he climbed that peak, he'd be willing to sit back for a while and enjoy the view for once. She doubted it, though.

"Is that why we were getting married?"

Will paused, his glass in midair. "It's not why I proposed to you, no."

"But it's why you stuck around even though I was difficult."

"We both had our reasons for getting married, even if they were misguided."

"I would think that it was just good business, working together. Why do you have to marry me to seal the deal?"

"It's not like that," Will insisted. "My proposal had nothing to do with your father's company. That all came later. Just an incentive to stick things out when you became—to use your word—*difficult*. Your father prefers to work with family. When I broke off our engagement, I did it knowing that this project could be dead in the water the minute he found out."

"If this second try doesn't work out between us, will it hurt your company?"

"No, it won't hurt us. But it won't help either."

"I could talk to him. I mean, I'm the reason we broke up. He shouldn't penalize you and your employees because of something I did."

"That's a very sweet offer, but I don't think I'm in need of any of your heroics just yet."

Will reached across the table to take her hand into his own. The warmth of him enveloped her and radiated up her arm like sinking into a hot bath. His thumb stroked across her knuckles in slow circles, sending the tiny hairs on the back of her neck to attention. She wanted to close her eyes and lose herself in the sensation of his touch, but his gaze had her pinned in her seat.

"What makes you think this second try won't work?" he asked with a devilish smile that almost convinced her it would.

Almost.

Five

"You *kissed* her?"

Alex's disbelieving shout no doubt cut through the walls of Will's office and into the hallways of the *Observer* headquarters.

"Keep it down, will you? I deliberately employ some very nosy people around here, and not all of them are journalists. My admin is at the top of the gossip food chain."

Will got up from his desk and pushed his office door closed, flipping the lock to prevent interruptions.

"What's the gossip in you kissing your fiancée?"

"Well, for a start, she isn't my fiancée anymore."

Alex sat down in Will's guest chair. "Yes, but only I know about the breakup. Last time we talked you seemed pretty certain you were out of there once she was back on her feet. What changed?"

Will sat down at his desk and leaned back, weaving his fingers behind his head. "Nothing. And everything."

"I knew it. I knew when I saw that grin on your face at dinner that she'd gotten to you."

Will wasn't sure he liked the implication of that, but he had a hard time denying that she'd gotten under his skin. "I've never been this preoccupied with a woman before."

"So you're staying?"

"No. Yes. For the time being. Even if she woke up tomorrow with the temperament of a pit bull, I'm riding this out until she's recovered. We've agreed to start fresh and see what happens, but I still have reservations. This just spells long-term disaster."

"Then why did you kiss her?"

Will sighed. "Because I wanted to. And I haven't really wanted to kiss her in a long time. There is suddenly this chemistry between us. This electricity whenever I'm close to her. It's nothing like we ever had before. It's as though I'm with a completely different woman. A brand new relationship with someone who's soft and sweet and gentle. I mean, she giggles, Alex."

A blond brow shot up, curious. "Cynthia giggled?"

"More than once. At first, she was sort of lost, trying to feel her way around, but now that she's got her bearings, she's full of excitement and joy. It's like she's got a new lease on life. I like being around her. I'm happy when she's happy. I bought her a damn sewing machine."

"What? Why?"

"Because I thought she'd like it, and I was right. She's cleared out her office of advertising junk and has been merrily plugging away at making clothes."

"Is that what she's going to do now?"

"I guess. She can't exactly go back to the ad agency and fake it. I encouraged her to do what inspired her, and this is the direction she took. It makes her happy."

Alex nodded. "Which makes you happy. So what's the big deal, then?"

"It's all wrong!" Will shouted, slamming his fist into his desk. Hitting something let out some of the aggression he had pent up inside. His gut was a swirling mix of untapped sexual energy, confusion and frustration with no outlet. "She's sucking me back in when all I wanted was to get out. It almost makes me wonder if she's doing it on purpose. When I broke it off, she was insistent that we could work things out. Cynthia didn't want the embarrassment of calling off the engagement. She wouldn't even take off her ring because she said we'd talk when she got home. What if she's trying to trick me into staying by faking this whole thing?"

"You mean pretending she has amnesia?"

"I wouldn't put it past her. I couldn't trust her then, and I'm still not sure I can trust her now. All she did was lie to me for more than a year."

"She nearly died in a plane crash. Not even Cynthia could premeditate a plan like that."

Will frowned at Alex, his argument instantly deflating because he knew his friend was right. He was being paranoid. Letting his past distrust of Cynthia cloud his judgment. Of course she couldn't have set this up, but somehow it was easier to be suspicious of her than to let himself trust her. "Ah, hell. What a mess I've made of things."

Alex stood and went over to the small bar where Will kept his stash of water, soda and Scotch. "Want a drink?" he asked.

"No, help yourself," Will said.

Alex poured himself a few fingers of Scotch and walked over to the large picture window that overlooked the vast concrete sea of New York City. "I think you've gone about this all wrong."

"Enlighten me."

The real-estate developer returned to Will's desk and sat back down in his chair. "You offered her a clean slate, but you're still letting all that old junk mess with your head. Let's take a page from Cynthia's book, so to speak. Forget about your past with Cynthia. Forget about this collaboration with Dempsey Corp. Even forget you were ever engaged."

Will looked at his friend with distrust. Those were a lot of factors to just sweep off the table. "O-*kay.*"

"Now," Alex continued, "with all that set aside, just ask yourself one simple question: Do you want her?"

Leave it to Alex to boil the situation down to base needs. But it made sense. Did he want her? Given that the blood pumped furiously through his body just from the sound of her laughter? Given that he'd locked himself in his office for hours with a miserable erection to keep himself from doing something stupid? "Yes."

"And with any other aspect of your life, what do you do when you want something?"

"I get it."

Alex shook his head. "You don't just get it, you tackle it. When you wanted to be student-body president, you campaigned like no one else. When you wanted to be the captain of the polo team in college, you worked harder than any other guy on the field. Cynthia could've had any man she wanted. But you set your sights high and you made her fall for you. You make things happen. It sounds like she's interested in you and you're interested in her. What's the problem?"

"It's not that simple. Yes, in your scenario it seems that way, but all those other issues still exist. I don't live in a vacuum."

"Yes, but what would it hurt if you guys gave this new relationship a solid try?"

Will knew the only thing that could get hurt was him, but that was only if he let it happen. Cynthia had the potential to really get into his head and into his heart, but he couldn't allow it to go that far. He didn't have a head injury to forget what Cynthia was capable of. But if he could keep his heart out of the equation, it would be better for business, and maybe he wouldn't mind coming home at night. "It wouldn't hurt anything," Will admitted.

Alex took another sip of his Scotch, a smug smile curling his lips. "Well, it's not my life, man, but if I were you, I'd go for it. March right out of this office and seduce the panties right off of her. Then enjoy it while it lasts. If she recovers and you hate each other again, so be it. You leave. You haven't lost anything that wasn't screwed before that plane went down."

"And if she doesn't recover?"

"They you'll live happily ever after. Simple as that."

It wasn't as simple as that, but it did give him something to think about. Will got up and poured his own small tumbler of Scotch.

Alex was right. He had told Cynthia he'd forgiven her, but deep down, he was still holding back. He hadn't committed himself the way he should've. And that wasn't fair to either of them. Will needed to let himself enjoy her, even if he couldn't let himself love her. Eventually something would ruin what they had, and he needed to take the chance while he still could.

Cynthia did the last bit of stitching and snipped the thread that ran from the cloth to the needle. She turned the dress right side out and shook it in front of her. It had taken her a few days, but her first piece was finished. She held it out to admire it and smiled. It wasn't bad.

She'd opted to start with the first design that called to her, regardless of whether it was too hard to tackle. It was a sleeveless shirtdress with a sort of fifties-era vibe. It buttoned down the front, with a sweet, rounded collar and a belt that tied at the waist. The skirt was full and fell just below the knee. She even considered constructing a crinoline underneath for fullness but opted to wait until it was finished to decide.

The silhouette was sophisticated, but it veered from the traditional with black-and-white zebra-printed fabric, splattered with hot pink and purple. The moment she saw the bolt of it sticking out of the racks, she knew it was the perfect choice for this project. She'd trimmed the edges and fashioned the collar and belt out of black satin that gave it a touch of shine and richness.

It was rockabilly meets the eighties. Funky, fun and unlike anything she'd seen people wearing. At least on the Upper East Side.

But now the real test. Slipping out of her clothes, she unbuttoned the dress and slipped it on. Turning and admiring it in the full-length mirror on the door, she was pleased and relieved to find she'd fitted it just right. After fastening the last button and tying the belt, the dress fit perfectly, flattering and forming to every curve.

It was just screaming for some black, patent-leather peep-toe sling-backs. Cynthia dashed down the hall to the bedroom and searched through shoeboxes until she found just the right pair. She slipped them on and then walked out into the living room to give the look a turn around the floor.

The sound of a loud cat-calling whistle made her spin on her heels.

Will was standing in the doorway, a look of open appreciation lighting his eyes. His heated gaze took in every inch of her, and she was fairly certain her skills at the sewing machine didn't have much to do with it. He smiled, shutting the door behind him. "Look at you," he said.

"Do you like it?" she asked, taking a twirl to make the full skirt swirl around her and torture him with the quick flash of bare thigh.

"I do," he said, swallowing hard. "I don't think I've ever seen anything like it."

"I just finished it a few minutes ago."

Will's eyebrows shot for the ceiling. "You mean you made that?"

"Yep. It's my first completed piece. I know the arm brace leaves something to be desired, but that will come off before too long."

"You went from a sewing-machine virgin to making a dress that is well constructed enough for the catwalk in three days? It took my little sister two weeks to figure out how to thread her machine when she took home ec. Her first dress looked like a purple potato sack."

Cynthia nodded. She'd had the same concerns when she first sat down. Fortunately, he'd bought her such a nice machine it practically ran itself. And sewing had simply come as second nature to her, which was frustrating considering how much of her previous life was a daily struggle. After reading over the manual once, the machine just made sense. Piecing together and pinning parts of the clothes on the dress form was easy. She might not know the name of every sewing doo-dad and gadget, but she would rummage through her things until she found what she thought would work. It was like she'd been doing it her whole life, which was impossible. And worrisome, honestly, if her joy of the new project hadn't taken precedence in her mind.

"I guess following my instincts has paid off. I'm really excited about making more. I was even thinking about making my dress for the party."

Will shrugged out of his coat and draped it over the arm of the sofa. "Ahh, yes. Your mother's soiree. It's the talk of the town. Choose your design carefully, as it might show up on the cover of every society paper and website in Manhattan."

Cynthia froze, mid-swish, her mouth falling slightly open. She hadn't thought about that. She kept forgetting that anyone gave a damn about what or who she was. There would be journalists there. Photographers. If she really wanted to be a designer, this would be the perfect launching board.

That, or they'd laugh her back to a figurehead VP job at her daddy's company. Who was she to just decide one day she wanted to do fashion? She had no training, no experience. Uncanny skill with a pencil and some scissors did not a career make.

"Maybe I should just stick with something in my closet, then," she conceded.

"Can't do that," Will said, closing the gap between them. "You can't be seen in something you've worn before. You've either got to buy a new dress or make one. And I think you should make one. Let everyone at that party know that Cynthia Dempsey has arrived, more fun and fashionable than ever."

Cynthia let her gaze drop from his, the compliment flushing her cheeks. "You're just being nice."

"No," Will said, standing directly in front of her and resting his hands on the small waist she accented with the cut of the dress. His fingers gently stroked her skin through the fabric, sending a warm awareness coursing through her veins. Her mouth went dry, her breasts tightening and aching to press against the hard wall of his chest.

Every time he got close to her, every time he touched her, she reacted this way. She just didn't understand. This couldn't be something new; this had to be chemistry and hormones at a base level. Something primitive. She couldn't squelch this reaction to Will even if she tried. And yet she had had an affair with someone else. She couldn't possibly feel this way and be with another man at the same time.

Will leaned in and pressed against her, and she was immediately pleased that she'd put on these high heels a moment before. The five-inch pumps put them on a level playing field. Mouth to mouth, chest to chest, hard length to soft belly.

"I believe I have my first fan," she said, her voice breathy and still slightly rough from the accident.

"Indeed." He leaned in and kissed her, capturing her mouth with unrestrained enthusiasm.

Cynthia met his advance with gusto. Their previous kisses, the way he touched her, had a hesitation like there was a war inside holding him back. Tonight there were no barriers. His tongue invaded her, his hands roaming across her body as though he were exploring new territory. She wrapped her arms around his neck, pressing her breasts against his chest and bringing his erection into direct contact with the sensitive juncture of her thighs.

Will moaned against her lips with the pleasure the pressure brought on. He slowly backed her against the living room wall and cupped one cheek of her ass, pulling her tighter to him. His lips traveled lightly across her jaw, still careful about the surgery she'd had, then moved down to feast on the sensitive curve of her neck. His hand drifted to encircle one of her breasts, his thumb stroking the hardened nipple that protruded through the fabric.

Cynthia gasped, the thrill of pleasure running down her back and exploding at the base of her spine into throbbing desire. She inched one thigh up the outside of his leg, hooking her knee around his hip. He pressed into her, the firm heat striking her sex. She couldn't contain her cry of pleasure. She'd never experienced a sensation like that before, and her body shuddered from the force of it.

Will continued sucking and biting at her neck, his fingers gently unfastening the chunky black buttons that held her dress on. Before she knew it, the top was undone to the waist and he was sliding his hands inside to caress her breasts through the thin lace of her bra.

Her breath caught in her throat as he left a trail of kisses down her neck to her collarbone and on to the valley between her breasts. He pushed aside the lace and took a hardened peak into his mouth, eliciting a strangled cry from her throat. Her fingers weaved into his hair tugging him closer. Now that she had him back in her arms, she didn't ever want to let him go.

Will's hand slid along her exposed thigh, pushing her dress higher as he moved. The tension in Cynthia's body increased with every inch, her body drawn tight as a drum. All her reservations about being with Will melted away. Nothing mattered but being in his arms right here, right now.

When his hand found the moist heat between her thighs, she thought she might explode with wanting him. His fingers stroked her gently through the silk of her panties, but it wasn't enough. Not nearly enough.

"Will, please," she whispered.

He pulled away from her breasts long enough to speak. "Please what? Tell me what you want, Cynthia."

A part of her flinched when he said her name. He'd said it a million times, but somehow saying it now, like this, brought the doubts back to her mind. She didn't want him calling her that. The concern was immediately wiped away by a tidal wave of pleasure as his finger made direct contact with her most sensitive spot.

"You," she managed, not quite sure she could form any other words.

Will's hand withdrew and she was about to revel in getting her way when she heard a soft ringing sound and realized he'd stopped because of the phone. She was about to chuck his stupid cell phone across the room when she realized it was the cordless phone on the table beside them. The caller ID was lit up with the last number in the world she wanted to see. He never called this late. There was no way she could hide the panic plastered over her face in that instant. No way she could pretend she didn't know who was calling.

Will pulled away, taking a full step back and leaving only her gelatinous legs precariously holding her up. When she looked in his eyes, the desire was gone, replaced only with the same cold indifference he'd had in the early days at the hospital. His jaw was tight, his face reddening slightly with an anger he refused to unleash even if she deserved it.

Instead, he turned and marched out of the room, slamming the apartment door behind him.

Completely deflated, Cynthia slid down the wall, her head cradled in her hands. With the phone still ringing, she picked it up from the cradle and threw it against the wall with a loud crack. The phone broke into several pieces, and that was enough to silence it, but the damage was already done.

Nigel had called again. And apparently Will recognized the number, too.

Six

By the time Will glanced down at his watch, it was after ten. He'd been pounding the pavement trying to figure out what to do. The cool night winds bit at his cheeks and forced his hands deeper into his pants pockets, but it barely registered in his brain as anything more than a nagging annoyance. He deserved the punishment for being that stupid.

He'd almost done it. Almost let himself go too far. Took Alex's ridiculous advice and set his inhibitions free. And what happened? Her lover called the apartment again.

Will could've let that go. Cynthia couldn't stop him from calling. But he'd hoped in that instant that she wouldn't recognize the number. That she would have the same blank look in her eye that she got when she met anyone else she should know and didn't.

But there was no denying the horror painted across her face. Cynthia knew exactly who it was. Knew exactly how poorly timed that bastard's call had been. His chest had grown so tight in that moment, he almost couldn't breathe.

He had to leave the apartment and get some fresh air before he suffocated.

She didn't remember her parents or her friends. Will, her fiancé of two years, was a total stranger. She didn't know if she liked hot dogs, for the love of God, but she remembered *him*. She'd even looked at Will, a glimmer of hope shining in her bright green eyes. Cynthia was hoping he didn't know who was on the phone. That he believed it when she said she wanted to put the past, and her lover, behind them. He was right not to trust her. The woman that betrayed him was still in there somewhere.

Spying an empty park bench, Will flopped down and decided to give his aching feet a break from their punishment. The shoes he wore to work weren't exactly designed for long strolls through the city. Hell, he was still wearing his suit minus the jacket he'd tossed aside. He'd accosted Cynthia the minute he walked in the door and then walked out without a second thought to how cold it was tonight. He hadn't eaten. Hadn't even checked his phone as it chimed and rang with repeated requests to contact him.

That plane crash was supposed to be their second chance. Her lover and all their other relationship baggage were supposed to be in the past. Just when he'd finally decided to take this chance seriously, she'd ruined it.

The blinking neon lights of the bar across the street from where he'd stopped beckoned Will to come in. He considered going inside and taking the edge off with some expensive whisky, but he knew drinking wouldn't help the situation. He was never one to just sit back and drown his sorrows. He always took action. And that was what he needed to do now.

Walking around Manhattan in the middle of the night wasn't going to fix anything. It helped him clear his head, kept him from doing something rash, but the only thing that could help him deal with this situation was probably asleep in their apartment.

Leaping back up after only a few moments rest, Will took the most direct route back to the apartment building. Cynthia had left on the entryway light, but the rest of the apartment was dark. He flipped on the living room lamp, illuminating the carnage that had once been their telephone. Based on the divot in the sheetrock, she'd slammed it against the wall.

Stepping around the plastic and metal bits, he continued down the hallway to their bedroom. He hadn't set foot into this space since the night she came home from the hospital. His clothes were in the closet of the guest room where he'd been sleeping, so there wasn't much point. He'd gathered his toiletries that night and had stayed out of her personal space while she adjusted.

Not tonight. Turning the doorknob, the light from the hall cast a beam across the king-size bed. He could barely make out the small bundle beneath the blankets. Will flipped on the lamp on his bed stand.

Cynthia was curled up tightly in the fetal position. She had tissue clutched in her hand and used tissues strewn over her nightstand. He could make out the dried tracks of tears across her cheeks. She'd taken it harder than he anticipated. She was so emotional lately.

"Cynthia," he said, shaking her arm softly so as to not startle her.

She muttered and shifted around, straightening out of her tight ball before her eyes fluttered open and her gaze fixed on him. They widened in an instant, and she shot up in bed even though he wasn't entirely certain she was fully awake. Her expression was panicked and confused, but as the fog of sleep faded away, her gaze hardened, protectively. She drew her legs up to her chest and scooted back against the headboard.

Will felt like a Goliath hovering over David, so he sat down on the edge of the bed and opted to face the wall so she wouldn't squirm under his gaze. "Why is Nigel calling again?" His voice was flat, unemotional. He didn't want her to shut down, and if he started yelling, she might.

"I don't know. He called the house the night I came home from the hospital while you were getting dinner. He kept talking to me like I knew who he was, but I didn't. It didn't take me long to figure it out, though." She shook her head and looked down at the tissue she was tearing to shreds in her hands. "He kept pushing to see me."

She looked back up at him, glassy tears sparkling in her green eyes. Seeing her cry was like an iron fist straight to his stomach. He wanted to reach out and soothe her, but he didn't react. For all he knew, this was a new tactic for manipulating him. He couldn't let her see that she was getting to him.

"Then I remembered what you said about choosing who I would be now. I couldn't do anything about what I'd already done, but I could put an end to it. So I told him I wouldn't see him and to stop calling."

Will's fists were curled tightly in his lap. He wanted to believe her, but a part of him had heard too many lies. "Why didn't you tell me? I thought we were starting over, being honest with each other?"

"I didn't want to drag it all back up. And he'd stopped calling at first. Then the calls started again. But I don't answer."

"I just don't know that I can trust you, Cynthia. I want to, but this doesn't help."

She flung back the covers and slid to the edge of the bed to sit beside him. She was wearing navy satin pajama pants with a matching tank top that left little to the imagination. The warmth of her hovered near, but not quite touching. His whole body hummed with the awareness of her, the scent of her skin making his brain lose focus. Will hated that even in this moment when he should despise her the most, he still wanted her. But he didn't pull away.

"You have no reason to trust me. And I have no reason to trust you. We're strangers. But I want more. I want this to work out. And I don't know of any other way to convince you of the truth."

Will looked down to see Cynthia slip off her engagement ring. She held it up and watched it sparkle in the light for a moment. "This isn't mine. You gave it to another woman. It's a symbol of our past and everything that has gone wrong between us."

Her fingers sought out one of his fists, uncurling it to place the ring in the palm of his hand.

"I know you're worried that one day I'll wake up and become *her* again. But you were right. I have a choice. Even if I recover my memory tomorrow, I'm promising you that I'm changing the person I was. I'd like to try making this work with you, with or without amnesia."

Since day one, Will knew her memory coming back would be the relationship killer. His interest and attraction to her would no doubt be erased by the return of her old personality. It was the thing he clung to, the last barrier he used to keep from letting himself get too close. And she'd just taken it away, leaving him exposed to her and their new possibilities together.

"Let's try to make a new relationship out of the wreckage of the one we destroyed. We can date, get to know each other as we are now. The world can continue to think we're engaged, including my father. And if and when," she said, her hand covering the one in which he held the ring, "you want to give that back to me…okay."

Cynthia watched Will's face for any sign that she wasn't about to be single and homeless, dragging two hundred pairs of shoes behind her down the street, but he was so hard to read. It wasn't until his other hand covered hers that she was able to take a breath.

"Okay," he agreed, although his face was still lined with concern. She understood that. She'd obviously hurt him.

Giving the ring back was evidence of her good-faith effort to make this work. In time, she hoped that they could make new memories to help mask the old ones. It would be a slow process, but she would take it one step at a time to be certain she did it right.

"I look forward to getting to know you," she said with a crooked smile and an awkwardly adolescent bump to his shoulder. "I like what I've learned so far."

His expression softened and he smiled, too. "It's been a long time since I've dated," he admitted. "I might be a little rusty."

"That's okay," she said with a shrug, "I don't remember ever going on a real date, so I'll be easy to impress."

At that, he laughed. It was the first real laugh she'd heard, and it was everything she hoped it would be. It was a deep, sexy rumble that vibrated in her chest and made her want to cling to him and bury her face in his neck.

"I'm glad your expectations are low," he said, turning to place a soft kiss on her lips. He pulled away immediately and stood up. "Good night."

She wanted him to stay, to pick up where they'd left off earlier, but she knew that wasn't the best idea. But the kiss held promise, just like their new relationship, and that was enough for her. "Good night," she said as he walked out of the room and then quietly pulled the door shut behind him.

Unfortunately, even as she switched off the lamp, she knew it was a lost cause. Sleep was no longer an option. She was as wired as if she'd chugged an entire pot of coffee. She'd gone to bed crying because she was certain she'd ruined everything. Now she had a world of new possibilities ahead of her. Her mind was spinning from their conversation, her thoughts bouncing around in her head. Cynthia lay there in the dark for nearly an hour, praying she would drift off to sleep, but it was no use.

She didn't have to get up early in the morning; she had nowhere to go, so she decided to put her energy to better use. Slipping quietly out of the bedroom and down the hallway to her workroom, she decided to do some sketching. She wouldn't run the sewing machine because the noise would wake up Will, but she could do everything else.

Her plan to make her own dress for her mother's party loomed heavy on her mind. It was an ambitious project to say the least, and she needed to start on it as soon as possible. Any design worthy of the event would be infinitely more complicated to construct than the dress she'd already made. It also needed to be well designed and perfectly suited to her style aesthetic. If it was going to be in newspapers, it needed to be the evening look she would use to close her collection on the runway. The wow piece that everyone could look at and say, "That's the latest Cynthia Dempsey design."

If that wasn't enough, she now had an added layer of pressure. She wanted to look good for Will, too. When she stepped out in this gown with her hair and makeup done, she wanted him to curse. She wanted him to threaten to rip it off her body and delay their arrival at the party—*if they arrived at all*—even though she was the guest of honor. To be honest, she wanted him to be as miserable with desire all night as she would undoubtedly be.

Will was a strikingly handsome man. Not pretty, like so many of the models in the magazines, but everything a man should be. Hard. Sophisticated. Confident. She'd seen him in everything from khakis to a suit, but she could only imagine how delicious he would look in his tuxedo. He had the broad shoulders and narrow waist that the jacket would cling to. His high, firm rear and solid thighs would be on display in his meticulously tailored suit pants. All he'd have to do is flash her one of his charming smiles and she'd be a puddle on the floor. Her best defense was a good offense, and she was going to make sure her new dress blew his mind.

Picking up her sketchbook, she flipped through pages to

see if any of the designs sparked her imagination. So far, she'd done a lot of casual wear and separates with a retro feel and modern styling. One of the sketches for a daytime dress caught her attention, and she knew that that was the piece she needed to use to transition the style into an elegant, formal look. The dress was fitted with a pencil-skirt silhouette and a sweetheart neckline that appeared to be like a corset atop a white dress shirt. It was a smart daytime look for the office.

Flipping to a blank page, she pulled out her colored pencils and started working on a new design. Like the daywear, this dress had a fitted silhouette, although instead of the skirt falling at the knee with a ruffled kick pleat, the gown would take it a step further by blooming into a full mermaid skirt. She echoed the neckline with a strapless sweetheart top that plunged deep in the center.

Losing herself in the sketch for an unknown amount of time, she added special details and penciled in the texture she hoped the fabric and beading she chose would provide.

Rubbing her eyes, she sat back from the picture and admired it with pride. Making this gown in time for her mother's party would be a challenge, but she could do it. The structure was actually easier to construct than sportswear. There was just one last decision to make—the color.

The theme of her collection had been a lot of black and white with pops of color. The dress would be stunning in black, but would it stand out enough? By the same token, she dismissed the bright pinks and teals other pieces had. That would be too much. Her gaze drifted over the pile of fabrics on the makeshift worktable that used to be a red sofa. It landed on a color she hadn't used yet, but that could easily be worked in. It was sure to be a stunner. She picked up the matching pencil off the table and started shading the dress, a smile curving her lips as she worked and brought the sketch to life. It was perfect.

Emerald green, just like her eyes.

* * *

Will found himself in the Flower District the next day after work. He hadn't been joking when he'd told Cynthia he was a little rusty where dating was concerned. He'd dated in high school and the first few years of college, but once he and Cynthia got together during their junior year, that was it. College girls hadn't required much wooing, and Cynthia had never been one for silly things like flowers and chocolates in the past. She wanted ice. He wouldn't have bought her an engagement ring guaranteed to get her mugged one day if she hadn't made it perfectly clear what she expected.

But now he had no idea what she expected. Well, actually he did. She expected very little, so any gesture would be welcome. That almost made it harder. He didn't want to slack off or not put in the effort she deserved because she was easy to please.

He picked up a bundle of roses. They were fresh and pink and reminded him of the color she blushed when he kissed her. Pink was her favorite color. Turning, he spied a few different types of lilies one stall down. Would she prefer something more exotic?

Will ran his fingers through his hair in exasperation and shook his head. He could only guess, so he opted to follow his instincts and go with his first choice. He walked to the counter, paid for the pink roses and hopped back in the cab that was waiting for him. Hopefully she would like them.

He rang the doorbell of their apartment when he got home instead of going inside. Her footsteps thumped across the floor as though she were running to the door.

"Did you forget your k—" she started as she flung it open, then she stopped when her gaze fell on the flowers in his hands. "Oh," she said, a smile lighting her face.

"I'm taking you on a dinner date this evening." He held out the flowers. "These are for you."

"Thank you," she said. "Let me put these in some water and I'll get ready."

Will nodded and followed her inside the apartment, shutting the door behind him. He watched as she searched the cabinets until she found a vase, unwrapped the flowers and arranged them in water before placing them on the kitchen table. "They're beautiful, Will, thank you."

"You're very welcome. I got us reservations for dinner at six-thirty. You'd better get a move on if we're going to make it on time."

Cynthia glanced at the clock and gasped, turning on her bare heels to disappear into the back of the apartment. Will waited patiently on the couch, wondering if she could manage to get ready that quickly.

Ten minutes later, he got his answer. She emerged from the back in a fitted black skirt and a ruffled white top with black details and stitching. She'd pulled her dark brown hair up into a bun and put on some lipstick that made her lips look pouty and plump like cherries. It was perfect.

"You look stunning," he said.

"Thank you. I tried to hurry."

"You did very well. We might even get there early."

They gathered their coats and caught a cab to the restaurant. It was an expensive Italian place, but not one of the society haunts where they might run into someone they knew. Not that she knew anyone. This being their first date, he wanted it to be private and without people gossiping about where they were and why her ring was suspiciously absent.

They were seated at a curved, burgundy leather booth for two, the table lit with the soft glow of candlelight. The sommelier brought him the wine list, and he was two seconds from ordering for her when he stopped. He didn't know what she liked anymore. "Do you want a diet soda, or would you like to try some wine tonight?" he asked.

She thought about it for a moment. "I'd like to try wine, but I want something light and sweet."

He nodded, taking the sommelier's suggestion for a brand of Riesling and a cabernet sauvignon for himself. Once they gave the waiter their order, they were finally left alone with a crusty loaf of bread and some herb-infused olive oil.

"Normally on a first date, I think I would ask a woman about herself, what she likes to do, where she grew up. Unfortunately, I don't think you know the answers."

Cynthia laughed and took a sip of her wine. "Mmm… this is lovely, thank you for choosing it. It might be hard, but maybe I can learn something about you *and me* while we're at it. Give it a try."

"Okay," he said, tearing a chunk of bread from the loaf and dipping it. "We'll go more esoteric, then. If you were trapped on a desert island, what three things would you take with you?"

"Well, if we're talking deserted with absolutely nothing, I say food, water and a toothbrush. If that kind of stuff is covered, then I say some books, a sketch pad with pencils and an mp3 player with a solar battery pack. How about you?"

"Given base needs are met, I would take…" he shook his head. "I almost can't even say. I wouldn't know what to do with a bunch of leisure time."

"What do you like to do for fun?"

"Fun? I just work. That's what I do. Occasionally Alex makes me play racquetball or you drag me to a party or a play. That's about it."

"Doesn't the paper own box seats at Yankee Stadium or something?"

"Courtside for the Knicks, actually, but I usually give the tickets out to clients and friends."

"Why? Don't you like basketball?"

"Yes. I just never make the time to go. You never wanted

to go with me, and Alex typically had a date or was traveling on business when I asked."

"When the season starts up again, I think I'd like to go. It sounds fun."

Will smiled as he tried to picture Cynthia at a Knicks game with a beer in one hand, nachos in the other, screaming at the players. "We can certainly do that. Anything else you'd like to try, assuming we go on a second date?" he said with a wink.

"Hmm…" She thought aloud. "Bowling, maybe. Or doing some of the touristy things around town. I don't remember any of that stuff, so it's like I'm a visitor."

"Do you mean like seeing the Statue of Liberty and Times Square?"

"Yeah. Maybe get one of those 'I ♥ NY' T-shirts."

Will had to laugh. The woman across the table from him surprised him every day. She really was an entirely different person. A sweet, caring woman with a zest for life and the simplest pleasures, like silly tourist fare. Maybe she really had changed for good. Enough that he could trust her with some of the feelings swirling in his gut but wasn't ready to say aloud.

"You know I work crazy hours, but I'll happily squeeze in some sightseeing with you if that makes you happy."

"It would. But tell me, why do you work so much?"

Will took a bite of bread to consider his answer. "When I took over for my father, Junior, after his retirement, it took a lot of hours to really get a feel for running the paper. Then things at home got strained and it was easier to bury myself in work. Then it just became a way of life."

"Isn't there someone else that can handle a lot of that stuff for you?"

He had a staff of hundreds of capable people, so he sincerely hoped so. "Probably, if I let them. But I like being involved. I don't want to be one of those disconnected CEOs in the ivory tower."

"There's got to be a happy medium. A line you can draw in the sand that says when you're working and when you're not. I mean, what would you say if I told you it was rude to constantly check your phone during our date?"

Will paused, his hand literally reaching out to compulsively check his phone when she spoke the words. His gaze narrowed at her and then he conceded with a nod. "I'd say you were probably right and offer to put it on silent." He held it up and flipped a switch, putting an end to the constant symphony of beeps, chirps and ringtone melodies. He wasn't comfortable turning it completely off in case there was a serious emergency.

"Well, that's a step in the right direction, I suppose. When was the last time you went on a vacation?"

"I took leave the Monday after your accident."

Cynthia frowned. "That's not a vacation. I'm talking sand between your toes and a frosty drink in your hand."

He thought back to his last trip and calculated how long it had been. "Sadly, it was after we graduated from Yale. Junior paid for both of us to spend a week in Antigua as a present."

"That was a long time ago. Do you have anything planned in the future?"

"Just our honeymoon. Two weeks in Bali," he said. "We reserved one of those little private huts over the water."

Will's mind instantly flashed to being on the beach with her. He knew she wasn't pleased with whatever weight she'd put on since the accident, but he didn't mind in the least. It gave a new fullness to her breasts and a roundness to her hips that would fill out a bikini quite nicely. He imagined rubbing thick, creamy sunscreen over every inch of her pale, delicate skin to protect it from burning. The undeniable desire to pull her into the water and taste the saltiness of her skin and the ocean mingling together washed over him. It was a fantasy worth indulging, even if not for a honeymoon. Two weeks in paradise, indeed.

"That sounds heavenly," she said, echoing his thoughts without realizing it. "Maybe we should plan something. Not necessarily two weeks in Bali, but something to get you away from work and me out of the apartment."

"Definitely," he said. Wherever it was, it had to have a beach, and he would buy her a pink bikini to wear. He'd already decided as much.

Just then, the waiter returned with their meals. "Wow," Cynthia remarked as she took in her large platter of pasta and immediately dug in. It provided him the luxury of watching her for a moment without her noticing.

Everything about Cynthia fascinated him. He supposed that having a brush with death could make you appreciate the smallest things, even fettuccine with clam sauce. It made him want to expose her to new things and shower her with gifts—not only because she deserved them but because she would genuinely appreciate them. He would take her on a tour of the city she would love, and as soon as the doctor cleared her to travel, they would be off to the nearest tropical locale. If she was too afraid to fly, he'd charter a yacht to take them there. But that would all come later.

First, he intended to expose her to another new experience. Once they got home, he was going to coax every type of pleasure he could from her body.

Seven

Cynthia could feel a change in the energy between them while they ate. At one point, she'd looked up from her food to find Will watching her intently. He'd barely touched his own meal, but the desire in his eyes made it obvious he was hungry for more than just pasta. She'd have to try tiramisu another night, because they were heading straight home after this course.

That was fine by her.

But as the elevator of their apartment building carried them up, Cynthia felt her nerves getting the best of her. She wasn't a virgin, but she felt as inexperienced as one. What was she supposed to do? She knew she was in capable hands with Will, but she wanted to please him, too. Hopefully he would understand and not think she was just bad in bed.

She also knew he probably couldn't help but draw comparisons from the past, and that worried her, too. Since none of her newer clothes fit, she knew she'd gained weight. Would he be disappointed to find that her body had changed? What if he wanted the lights on? Cynthia wasn't sure she was brave enough for that yet.

Will took her hand and led her from the elevator to their door. She let him guide her inside. He locked the door behind them, tossed his keys onto the table where the phone used to be and made his way into the living room.

When he reached up to turn on the light, Cynthia caught his hand. "How about just the fireplace?" she suggested. Even that light was too much, but she didn't want to sound immature. The fire would still cast shadows, and the dim glow would mask the imperfections she hoped to hide.

He nodded silently, going through the motions of starting a fire and gesturing for her to sit on the thick area rug in front of the fireplace. She kicked off her shoes and sat down to watch him. With the flames started, Will disappeared into the kitchen and returned a few minutes later with two flutes of champagne. "Have you tried champagne yet?"

"No," she said as she accepted the glass and watched him lower to the rug beside her.

"Then, to the first of several new experiences tonight I hope you'll enjoy." Will held up the flute and clinked it with hers.

Cynthia could feel herself starting to blush and hoped the fireplace didn't make it too obvious. She brought the glass to her lips and took in a sip of the sweet, bubbly drink. It was wonderful. She took another large sip. The fizz seemed to go straight into her veins, warming her whole body and relaxing the muscles that tensed as he lingered close.

"Do you like it?" Will asked, setting his half-empty flute on the nearby coffee table and then leaning closer to her.

"I do." She swallowed the last bit for a dose of liquid courage and set it aside.

"Good." He reached out to cradle the nape of her neck and leaned in to close the small gap between them. His lips met hers, and she instantly felt lightheaded in a way that had nothing to do with champagne. His mouth was warm and tasted sweet against hers. The feel of his fingertips massaging through her hair coaxed her eyes closed, and she gave in to the sensation of him.

She felt the heat of his hand on her thigh. It stroked gently through the fabric of her skirt, slowly inching it higher up her leg. The caress lit a fire deep in her belly that urged her to reach out to him. Cynthia pressed a hand against his chest, kneading at the hard muscles, but the starched fabric of his dress shirt didn't feel good against her palms. She wanted to touch bare skin. Starting at his collar, she worked at the buttons, pausing as she reached his waistband. There, the brush of her fingertips across his stomach elicited a deep groan of approval against her lips. It made her bolder, and she tugged his shirt out and undid the last button, slipping the shirt over his shoulders and exposing his chest.

This, she wanted to see. Pulling away from his kiss, she opened her eyes and took in the hard expanse of his chest, the ridges and planes of his body accented and shadowed by the flickering fire. It beckoned her to reach out, and she indulged. She reveled in the velvet glide of her fingertips across his skin. The muscles of his stomach jumped as her hand neared his navel, and Will shot a hand out to grasp her wrist. "Not yet," he whispered, moving her hand higher to rest on his shoulder.

Will kissed her again, and this time she could feel his hands move down her blouse, opening it as she had done to his shirt. For a moment her nerves returned, but her back was to the fire, so when he eased her blouse off, her chest was still cloaked in shadow. His hand slid like satin over her exposed back, grasping the catch of her bra and undoing it with a flick of his fingers. Without his mouth leaving hers, he slid the bra down her arms and tossed it aside, covering the aching globes of her breasts with his greedy hands.

Cynthia gasped against his lips as he pinched one hardened peak between his fingertips and then soothed the ache with his palms. The sharp sensation traveled straight to her inner core, urging her body forward to press against him, but it wasn't nearly enough to soothe the need building inside her.

Will unzipped her skirt at the hip and surged forward, easing her back until she was lying flat on the rug. The movement exposed her body to the glow of the fire, but when she caught him looking down at her with unbridled lust, her heart leapt in her chest. For a moment, she was able to put aside all her insecurities and bask in the glow of being truly desired. It was a new and wonderful feeling, second only to the tingle of his lips against her skin as he traveled down her exposed chest. His mouth captured one tight nipple while his hands moved lower to tug her skirt and panties down over her hips. Only when he absolutely had to did his mouth leave her body, and that was only to cast the last of her clothing, then his, aside.

Cynthia sat up on her elbows and tried to admire what she could of his body, but her plan to disguise her own insecurities had made it hard for her to see him, as well. She could only see the shadow of his body moving, hear the crinkle of a foil packet tearing open, then see the golden light on his brown hair as his body slowly moved toward her. His hands and mouth stroked and tasted every inch of her as he glided up to cover her body with his own, shifting his weight to rest on his hip and elbow alongside her.

His dark gaze fixed on her as his flat palm grazed over her belly and then dipped between her thighs. He eased her open to him and then let his fingers glide over her moist flesh. Cynthia tried not to cry out, but the sensations overwhelmed her and she simply couldn't help it. She fought to keep her eyes open and hold the connection, but the expert movements of his hand sent her eyelids shut and her hips rising up to meet his touch. The electric current of pleasure running through her body was like nothing else she'd ever experienced before. The pressure was building up inside of her, making her achy and hungry for more.

"Will," she whispered, her body no longer her own to control as he coaxed new feelings out of her. She couldn't imagine feeling anything more incredible than this moment, but she knew there was more. She wanted all of him and would feel incomplete until she did. "Please."

Nudging her thighs farther apart, Will settled in and hovered over her. His gaze never left hers as he rocked forward and found his home within her welcoming body. He filled her so completely that she gasped; the pleasure was almost more than she could bear. She'd waited so long for this, she wanted to lock her legs around him and keep him there forever.

But even she wasn't stupid enough to stop the delicious movement he'd begun. It was slow at first, inch by inch easing in and out of her body at an excruciating pace. His head dipped down to capture a nipple in his mouth and tug at it with his teeth.

"Oh, Will," Cynthia said, unable to do anything else but cling to the hard muscle of his arms. The climax was building inside her, but it was too soon. Far too soon. She wanted this feeling to last forever, and he wasn't going to allow it.

He released her breast and kissed her, the salty taste of her skin on his lips. She clung to him as he moved faster, thrusting inside her with increasing force. Every second brought another rush of pleasure, her nerve endings almost unable to take any more.

He seemed to enjoy watching the expressions on her face as her mouth fell open, her chest rising and falling with the rapid breaths of her oncoming orgasm. With perfect timing, he thrust home harder and harder, pushing her off the cliff until she had no choice but to dive into oblivion.

"Yes!" she cried out as the climax pulsed through her body. Her hips bucked against his driving pelvis, her back rising off the rug as her release exploded inside her. She got lost in the tide of ecstasy, her cries mingling with his as he found his own release.

Cynthia collapsed back into the carpet, Will throwing his leg to one side to put the bulk of his weight off her. They lay there together, a mix of heavy breathing and tingling bodies. That was the most incredible thing she'd ever experienced. Being in Will's arms, connecting with him like that, brought not only pleasure but a sense of peace she'd been lacking. She didn't delude herself into believing this was anything more than incredible sex to Will, but it was a start. If and when they finally made love, she imagined it would be even better. For tonight, she would let herself be happy with a successful first date.

Their first date. "So much for my reputation," she said, laughing as best she could manage between her harsh, ragged breaths.

Will tapped gently against the door to Cynthia's workroom and called her name. He heard the loud stitching of the sewing machine stop.

"Yes?" she said, her voice muffled by the heavy wood between them.

"We're going out tonight," he announced. She had been holed up in her workroom for days. They were going out whether she liked it or not. He didn't care if she went to the party in half a dress.

"I don't think I—" She began to argue, but he grabbed the doorknob and silenced her protest. "No, no, I'm coming!"

She flung open the door and quickly pulled it shut behind her. "No peeking," she reminded him with a frown.

"You've been working too much, and coming from me, that's pretty bad. I'm taking you out tonight."

"I really shouldn't," she said, backing into the room again, but his hand shot out to grab the door and keep her from re-treating.

"If you go back in there, I will come in after you and carry you out. After I thoroughly examine your dress and ruin the surprise."

Cynthia glanced down at her raw and bloody fingertips and gave a resigned sigh. "I could probably use some time away. I'm making progress, though."

"That's great." Will slipped out of his sport coat and headed down the hallway to the guest room. "I'm going to change before we leave." He pulled off his shirt and tie, throwing them on the bed.

"I guess I should, too. Where are we going?"

"It's a surprise," he called out.

"Then how will I know what to wear?"

Will stepped back into the hallway and eyed her outfit. She had on low-ride jeans and a T-shirt, her hair down and loose around her shoulders. For what he had in mind, it was perfect. He was about to tell her as much when her mouth dropped open and a gasp of surprise escaped her throat. He looked down at his bare chest in confusion and then back to her red cheeks. They'd slept together only two nights ago, but apparently seeing him in full daylight was a whole new experience for her.

He was glad his abs met with her approval. His lips twisted in amusement for a moment before he spoke. "Stop that or we'll never leave the apartment. You look fine. Just put on a jacket and some comfortable shoes."

Cynthia's eyebrows shot up, but she didn't argue. She went into the master bedroom and reappeared a few minutes later wearing her jacket and with her running shoes laced up and ready to go.

He met her in the hallway wearing jeans, a gray polo shirt and his own pair of sneakers. It had been a long time since he'd worn jeans and sneakers. He forgot how comfortable they were.

She followed him to the door and he slipped into his leather jacket. "I take it we're not going to *Le Bernardin* tonight?"

"Nope." Will ushered her out of the apartment and down the hall.

"I have to admit, I'm a touch relieved. I'm too tired to worry about keeping my elbows off the table and which fork to use."

"I'm glad you approve."

"Any clues?" she asked in the elevator.

"Nope."

There was a touch of frustration in her eyes, but it was quickly erased with the light of excitement.

First, they hopped in a cab and he took her to a small underground pizza joint near the Theater District. He could tell by the look on her face that she was hesitant about it. The first time he'd walked in, he thought he might need a tetanus shot, but it was some of the best pizza in town. By the time she'd put away her second giant slice, he was pretty sure Cynthia would agree.

Then they walked a few blocks to 42nd Street. Every time they approached the entrance to a theater, she'd look around expectantly, but he would continue on past. No Broadway musicals tonight. Instead, he'd bought tickets to a Night Illuminations tour. When the giant double-decker bus rolled up, Will knew he'd made the right choice. Her face lit up immediately. The air was chilly on the top deck, but Will didn't mind. It gave him an excuse to wrap his arm around Cynthia so she could snuggle against his side. She asked him questions about sights they passed and he told her all he could. He'd always thought the lights of the city were beautiful, but sharing them with Cynthia made them even more special.

After about two hours, they'd seen all of Manhattan and

the tour dropped them back near Times Square. While she was mesmerized by a billboard, Will surprised her with an "I ♥ NY" T-shirt and a pretzel with mustard. They walked around for a while, and when she was nearly finished eating, she forced him into the four-story Toys "R" Us store to ride the indoor Ferris wheel.

It was an experience he would've skipped normally, but her excitement was contagious. "You had to pick the My Little Pony car, didn't you?" Will said as they stepped back out into the night. "We couldn't ride in the Monopoly car or even the Mr. Potato Head one."

"Is there something wrong with riding in a pink-and-green pony cart with rainbows and clouds?"

"Not if you're a five-year-old girl," he snorted.

"Where's your sense of adventure?"

Will stopped at a street corner and waited for the light to change before taking her by the hand and leading her to the other side. "I must've left it in my other pants."

"Speaking of which," Cynthia noted, "I like you in jeans. You look a lot more relaxed than you do in those power suits."

Will looked down at his outfit and shrugged. He was more relaxed, although he doubted his pants were the cause. He'd made the decision earlier in the night to turn his phone off. Before he left work, he informed his admin and his second in command, Dan, that he would be "unplugged" tonight. It was time Dan started earning his deputy title. It was hard to actually hit the power button, but within minutes, he could almost feel his blood pressure go down.

"I think it has more to do with the fact that I turned my cell phone off."

"Not just silent? Actually off?" Cynthia nearly choked on her last bite of pretzel.

"Yes, off." He was surprised she hadn't noticed, since it was constantly making noise, but with the honking cabs and tourist crowds, she might not have heard it, even with it on.

"What's that all about?" she asked, looking up to admire the sea of neon lights that surrounded them.

"You said I work too much. So I'm trying…something. It doesn't stop me from looking at the blank screen periodically out of habit, but it's a first step."

Cynthia broke into a wide smile. "Before long, I'll have you taking vacations and enjoying life outside the office." She turned to face him and reached up to wrap her arms around his neck. "I appreciate the effort. I know how important the *Observer* is to you."

He shrugged. "It is, but people are important, too. I'm trying to relax. Trying to enjoy my time with you." Will looked down at her, her eyes reflecting the neon. His hands had been resting on her hips, but now they snaked around her waist to pull her tight.

Cynthia eased up onto her toes and closed the distance between them for a kiss. The moment their lips met, the sounds of the city faded away. There was only the feel of his hard chest pressed against her soft one, the sweet taste of her mouth and the warmth of her skin.

Will felt exposed standing on the sidewalk. He slowly eased Cynthia backward into an alcove in the façade between stores and pressed her back into the wall.

Now they had the freedom to let their hands roam. Her palms flattened against his chest, feeling and exploring. Her fingernails scratched at his skin through the cotton of his shirt, eliciting a growl from deep in his throat.

Will leaned against her until her soft body molded to every hard inch of him. She gasped when he pressed his arousal into her belly and he closed his eyes to block out everything but the sensation of it. His tongue glided across hers, his hand daring to slide up her side under her jacket to stealthily cup her breast through the thin cotton of her T-shirt.

"Excuse me."

His eyes flew open as he took a step away from Cynthia.

They both turned and found one of the city's mounted police officers standing nearby. He looked down at them and shook his head as though he were expecting teenagers, not full-grown adults that could afford to do this at home.

"Times Square is a family place these days," he said. "Why don't you find a room somewhere?"

"Yes, Officer," Will said as he attempted to mask the grin on his face.

The policeman tipped his hat and signaled to the horse to continue its path down the sidewalk.

Will turned to her, pressing her back against the wall, but not daring to kiss her again. If he started, he doubted he'd be able to stop a second time. "We'd better go home before you tempt me to do something to get us both arrested." He spied a cab dropping someone off on the curb and waved it down.

Cynthia smiled and silently arched her back to grind against him one last time.

Will gritted his teeth together to keep a grip on his rapidly eroding control. "Get in the taxi, you minx."

Eight

The past few days, while passing in a blur, had been an exercise in restraint that Will could've done without. With the party looming close, Cynthia had become like an art exhibit in the Met. All he could do was admire her from a distance. He'd had a taste of her and he wanted more. With every day that passed by, the need within him built. Abstinence made the heart grow fonder, he mused.

They'd made a ritual of eating breakfast together in the morning before he left for work and she disappeared into her workroom. When he got home, he'd lure her away from the sewing machine for dinner. Once the dishes were cleared, she was back in her office working on her dress, despite his halfhearted attempts to lure her away. He was certain that if he'd been determined he could've succeeded, but he understood her drive. This dress was important to her like his paper was important to him. She wanted to do her best, and he didn't want to distract her.

That didn't mean he didn't lie in bed each night listening to the sewing machine whirr and ache to hold her. Fortunately, his celibate streak was coming to an end. Tonight was the party, and Cynthia's masterpiece would be revealed.

He slipped the last onyx stud through the buttonhole, adjusted his tie and shrugged on his black tuxedo jacket. Will glanced at his reflection in the mirror one last time, but things were as good as they were going to get.

Cynthia, however, had been in her bathroom for over an hour. He'd heard the water run, the blow-dryer and then a long silence where she was doing God knows what. He was glad he didn't have to worry about makeup and fussy hairstyles. He'd stopped in for a haircut earlier in the week and shaved after his shower, and that was about it.

He glanced at his watch and was pleased that they seemed to be on time so far. A limo would be picking them up downstairs in just a few minutes. Gathering his things, he sat on the couch to wait for her.

It didn't take long. The clicking of her heels on the hardwood in the hall caught his attention a moment later. Will looked up as she entered the room and nearly choked.

There were really no words for how amazing she looked. He rose to his feet, his mouth open but at a loss for what to say. Apparently that was good enough for Cynthia, who smiled and gave a turn in her gown. The dark green dress shimmered as the light hit the beads. It hugged every curve of her body, the neckline dipping down just enough to give him a luscious view of the swell of her breasts.

Across her bare neck, she wore an emerald necklace he'd bought for her when she'd made partner at her agency. The intricate gold design had nearly twenty emeralds inset into it, with the largest a teardrop that hung tantalizingly into her cleavage.

But none of it sparkled like she did. Her dark hair was twisted up off her neck with gold combs. Wearing her hair back let the pale beauty of her face shine. The matching emerald earrings dangled from each ear and brought out the brilliant green and gold in her eyes. She'd done her makeup perfectly with smoky colors that made her look sexy and mysterious.

She was simply stunning. He knew she worried about not looking precisely like she had before the accident, but her brilliant smile and personality made her glow more radiantly than she ever had before. The doctor had cleared her to remove the brace, so the chunky gold bracelets on her left arm hid the scar. Anyone who met Cynthia for the first time tonight would never know she was anything less than perfection.

"Gorgeous," he managed with a smile. "And the dress ain't bad either."

"Thank you," she said, her cheeks blushing with the compliment. For the first time he noticed her blush ran down her neck to her chest as well, turning the tops of her breasts an attractive pink color beneath the gold necklace. He wanted to run his tongue along the swell of her rosy flesh and bury his face into the deep valley between them.

Shifting uncomfortably as the fly of his tuxedo pants pressed into his arousal, he decided that focusing on her breasts was probably the wrong tactic if they were going to get through the next few hours. "Are you ready?"

"I am." Cynthia scooped up a small black purse and her wrap off the table.

Will offered her his arm as they walked out of the apartment and down to the lobby. Alone in the dark, private recesses of the limousine, he said, "You really do look dazzling. It's going to take everything in my power not to peel this dress off of you before we get to the party."

She smiled and turned to him. "Do I need to slide over and give you some space?"

"Don't you dare." His voice was a low growl as he slipped one arm around her back, the other gliding over her hip to actually press her closer. He wanted to pull her into his lap. To see her lipstick smeared across his stomach. How on earth would he be able to wait four or five hours to have her? He'd quickly become addicted to the woman in his arms.

"Could I offer you a little something to tide you over?"

Will arched an eyebrow at her. "What do you have in mind?"

She smiled and placed a hand on his cheek. "For now, just a kiss. Something to keep in your mind tonight when you're bored to tears and ready to leave."

Cynthia lifted her mouth to him. Her lips were soft against his, her mouth opening slightly. She tasted like peaches, he thought, realizing she must have some kind of flavored lip gloss on. It was intoxicating to drink her in as she deepened the kiss and let her silken tongue glide along his own.

He let her take the lead, knowing in his present state of mind, he'd take it too far and ruin Pauline's plans. He kept his hands firmly around her without roaming. But it was very, very difficult.

All too soon, she pulled away. "You're going to need more of that peachy stuff," he said with a strained smile.

"Thanks," she said, turning to her purse for her compact.

By the time the limo came to a stop outside the hotel, her lips were perfect and shiny and he had quelled the raging erection that wouldn't allow him to get out of the limo. She'd given him something to think about tonight, all right, but it was too dangerous a thought around all those other people.

Once they reached the party, it was absolute chaos. Dignified, well-dressed chaos, but a ruckus nonetheless. Cynthia's parents were greeting everyone as they came through the door of the ballroom, and her arrival was the official kickoff of crazy.

Will got the feeling that Cynthia had hoped to slip in unnoticed and get acclimated first, but the chances of that dissolved in an instant when Pauline announced her arrival to the entire room. He could feel her stiffen beside him as she was approached by person after person. They were all very sweet, fully aware of her condition and introducing themselves, but it was still an overwhelming sea of strangers for her. She held a tight grip to his arm, so he knew not to disappear and talk shop with any of the other publishing types he saw milling around the bar. He wasn't in the mood to do business anyway.

"Oh, Cynthia," one woman nearly shrieked as she came forward to embrace the reluctant amnesiac. "You look absolutely beautiful, darling. Oh," she continued on in a chatter when Cynthia stared blankly at her, "I'm sorry, I forgot. I'm Darlene Winters. I work for *Trend Now* magazine as the senior fashion editor. We've worked together for years on ad campaigns for the magazine."

Cynthia nodded, but he could tell she had a new type of nerves getting to her. A woman like Darlene Winters could kick-start her dreams of designing clothes, and she knew it.

"Let me look at you, darling," Darlene said, taking a step back. "That dress is absolutely stunning on you. Who are you wearing?"

Cynthia's mouth came open to speak, but nothing came out. Panic started creeping into her green eyes, so Will stepped in to intervene.

"You are looking at a Cynthia Dempsey original, Darlene. She designed and made this dress herself."

Darlene didn't have the kind of face that moved much after years of Botox and facelifts, but even then you could detect the expression of surprise. "Are you designing now? That's fabulous."

Will nudged Cynthia to respond. "Yes," she said, her voice quiet at first but growing more sure as she spoke. "I'm working on my first collection. This gown is the centerpiece. I'm very proud of it."

"You should be, honey. Listen, I don't want to take up all

your time, this is your party, but give me a call. I'd love to get together with you next week and take a look at what you're working on. This dress has me salivating for more."

Cynthia nodded and waved her hand casually as Darlene disappeared into the crowd. "Did that just happen?" she whispered to Will.

"Yep," he said with a smile. He turned to her and leaned down to plant a soft kiss on her peach lips. "Don't be afraid to tell people about your work. It's brilliant, and they should all know it."

She smiled up at him, her eyes glistening with tears of excitement and overwhelming emotion. This dream had quickly become very important to her. So it was important to him. He would support her in whatever way she needed.

The orchestra started playing a popular tune, and several of the people around them disappeared to pair off on the dance floor. He needed at least one good drink before he was loose enough to attempt that, so he decided to take advantage of the suddenly shorter line for the bartender.

"Let's go get a drink," he said. "It will make this easier for us both."

When they approached the bar, Will recognized the shaggy blond hair of the man in front of them. "Alex?" he said as he slipped his arm around Cynthia's narrow waist and snugly tugged her against his side for safekeeping.

Alex turned with a brand new drink in hand. "Hey, Will," he said, shaking his hand and then turning to look at Cynthia. His hazel gaze raked over her for a moment, lingering a second longer than Will liked on the plunge of her dress. He knew his friend had a hard time mentally switching out of playboy mode.

"Cynthia," he said with a smile, and just like that, he squelched the stalking panther and turned on the boyish charm that made him the favorite of older ladies everywhere. "You are looking mahh-velouss," Alex overexaggerated, leaning in to give her a kiss on the cheek. "You are a goddess at the sewing machine," he added.

Cynthia blushed and Will fought the need to pull her closer to him. His friend was harmless. He knew Alex had a strict code, and infidelity and seducing a friend's woman, even an ex, was a violation. Cynthia was safe. Every other woman in the room, however...

"Cyndi?"

Will's thoughts were interrupted by the arrival of Cynthia's sister, Emma. The teen was grinning with excitement, apparently having reached the age where Pauline would not only let her attend a party but wear a fancy dress and makeup, too. She was a pretty little thing who looked a lot like her sister, with flawless pale skin, high cheekbones and shiny, dark hair. The braces were probably a godsend, letting everyone know, including guys like Alex, that despite her tiny dress and attempt at being a grown-up, she was still jailbait.

A few more years and Emma would be out on the town giving George and Pauline heart palpitations.

Cynthia smiled and hugged her sister, letting the teen pull her away for a few minutes to talk about girly things, he supposed.

"I see you've charmed those panties off," Alex said, leaning in with a sly grin.

Will shook his head with a sigh. "You're awful. But if you don't mind me asking, how did you know?"

Alex took a sip of his drink and eyed Will with a mix of amusement and concern. "You're in serious trouble, man."

He frowned and turned to his friend, grateful Cynthia was distracted by her sister for a moment. "Trouble?"

"Yep. She's got you. I can see it when you look at her. I'd say you're one step away from being completely lost."

Will took a sip of his own drink, hoping the alcohol would muffle the alarm bells his friend's words had set off. He was giving this a second chance, but he thought he was being especially cautious to not rush into something he would regret. "Don't be ridiculous."

Alex slapped him on the back, a wide smile lighting his face. "I didn't say you should fight it, man. There's nothing quite like being completely lost to a beautiful woman. You look really happy with her. I just hope you let yourself enjoy it for once."

Before Will could answer, Alex gave him a wink, waved to Cynthia and disappeared into the crowd, back on the prowl.

After an hour or so, Cynthia finally got brave enough to leave Will's side and explore on her own. She'd had a few drinks and hors d'oeuvres, allowed her parents to take her around and introduce her to a million people and then sat through a miserable round of speeches in her honor.

But now she was alone, standing unnoticed near the edge of the crowd and sipping a glass of wine to help her unwind. It was all very overwhelming.

A man's hand reached for Cynthia's elbow, tugging her gently behind a decorative fabric panel in the ballroom. Perhaps Will's determination to resist ravishing her was wearing thin. She allowed herself to be lured away, setting down her glass, but she stopped short when she realized the man touching her was not Will.

She recognized Nigel from the photos in her office, although he didn't look nearly as happy as he had on the beach. His large, brown eyes reflected the same anger that was etched into every inch of his unshaven jaw. He had messy, dark blond hair and an ill-fitting tuxedo that was obviously rented at the last minute. In the photos, he'd had a bit of rugged, boyish charm, but at that moment, she wasn't entirely sure what she ever saw in him.

"Aren't you looking fancy tonight?" he said with a mocking tone. "That necklace alone could pay for three years of rent on my studio in the Bronx."

"Take your hand off me," she said, her voice as cold as she could manage.

"No way in hell, sweetheart. If I do, you'll run back to your rich fiancé."

"I told you on the phone that I had no idea who you were and had nothing else to say to you." She tugged, but his fingers pressed more cruelly into her upper arm. "How did you even get in here?"

"I used my last hundred dollars to rent this tux and bribe the doorman." Nigel smiled, apparently pleased with his ingenuity.

"Why? What do you want?"

His dark eyes pinned her and made her squirm uncomfortably. "I want the woman I love back."

"The woman you loved died in that plane crash. I may have physically lived through it, but I'm a different person now."

"So, you think you can just cast me aside because I'm not William Reese Taylor the Third?" he said with a sarcastic sneer that curled his upper lip. "You said you loved me."

Cynthia watched a touch of sadness creep into the man's dark eyes. They'd had something together, something that was still important to him. And for that she had some sympathy. But Will was important to her and she wasn't going to screw up her second chance.

"I don't know what kind of relationship you and I had, but believe me when I say it's over. Regardless of what I've said or promised you in the past, we're done. I'm working things out with Will."

She could feel rage coursing through his veins, the iron grip on her arm not lessening for even a moment. She was going to have a miserable bruise if he wasn't careful.

"You're going to regret using me, Cynthia." At that, he let go of her and stomped to the exit.

There was something about his tone that made her glad her building had a twenty-four-hour doorman. Once the door slammed shut, Cynthia flopped back against the wall with a rush of relief. She brought her hands up to cover her face so no one could see the horrified mix of fear, sadness and gratitude that he was gone. Taking a deep breath and running her hand over her upper arm to soothe where he'd gripped her, she painted on her best smile and melted back into the crowd. She moved immediately to her abandoned drink, swallowing a large sip of it and setting down the glass before someone saw how badly her hand was shaking.

"Pumpkin?"

Cynthia didn't get her wish. She turned toward the voice and found her father coming toward her with a look of concern on his face. "Yes, Daddy?"

"What was that all about? Do I need to call security?"

That was the last thing she wanted. The less attention drawn to this the better. "No, not at all. It was nothing."

Her father's sharp gaze focused on the red splotch Nigel left on her upper arm. "That sure looks like something to me."

"It's just a misunderstanding. I'm fine. Where's Mother?"

He shrugged, allowing her to put an end to that conversation. "I left her talking to that obnoxious woman from the country club. That always ends up being expensive."

Cynthia nodded, her nerves over the argument with Nigel slowly starting to fade. "I'm going to find Will. I'm hoping I can convince him to take me home. I'm exhausted. You'd better rescue Mother before you end up owning a house on Martha's Vineyard."

"All right," he said, leaning in to give her a big hug. "If you need me to take care of that, all you have to do is call," he whispered into her ear.

"You sound like a mobster, Daddy." She pulled away and smiled. "Everything is fine, really."

"Okay. You look beautiful tonight, pumpkin. I hope you

had a good time." He kissed her on the cheek and reluctantly stumbled off in search of his wife.

Alone again, she went to the bar and got herself a new glass of white zinfandel, which she could hold without shaking uncontrollably. Taking another sip, she closed her eyes, swallowed and took a deep breath. She needed to get a grip.

"There you are." Will's voice whispered close to her ear, his breath warm on her neck.

She spun in his arms to face him. "Hello," she said, pasting a smile on her face. "Are you having fun?"

He shrugged. "I've never really cared for these kinds of things. This party is for you, so naturally it's the best party ever thrown, but I'd just as soon rush you out of here and find out what's under that dress."

There was a heat in his cool blue eyes that promised he would make good on every word. The warmth of his hands on her sunk deep into her body, and the worries of a moment ago seemed to disappear. He had such a powerful effect on her. Having him so close, his cologne and warm male scent tickling her nose, was enough to make her want to rub against him and purr like a cat. She was about to suggest he take her home when he looked down at this watch.

"I guess we can't avoid it any longer."

Cynthia frowned in confusion. "Avoid what?"

"The dance floor. Come on," he said, taking a step back and holding out his hand to her. "We've got to take at least one lap around the floor before we leave. Pauline paid way too much for the orchestra for us not to."

"I don't think I know how to dance," she confided as he led her through the crowd. It was part of the reason she hadn't brought it up earlier. She'd rather look lovely in the crowd then stand out for looking foolish.

"Don't worry, I'm no Fred Astaire."

They made their way to the center of the floor where a large group of couples had already gathered. Will took Cynthia's hand in his, wrapped his arm around her waist and pulled her tightly against him. "We'll keep it simple," he said with a smile.

It was a good thing he meant what he said, because she could hardly think this close to him. The whole length of her body was pressed into his as they glided around. The song was slow and the steps were easy, but she hardly noticed anything but her handsome dancing partner.

"I'm going to have to keep a better eye on you tonight," Will whispered into her ear after a few minutes.

Cynthia felt her chest tighten but tried not to let the panic show in her eyes. Instead she turned to place her head on his shoulder so he couldn't see her face. "Why is that?" she asked. Had he seen Nigel?

"Because every eye in this room is on you, and every man here is drooling over how your dress looks like you were poured into it." His hand slid lower on her back to rest just above the flare of her hips. The heat sank into the base of her spine, a warm tingle starting there and working its way through her body.

Perhaps Nigel hadn't ruined tonight after all. "Mmm-hmm…" she murmured, her heart not slowing as the worry subsided but increasing with his caress. Her whole body was on high alert and aching for more of him. The few days she'd gone without his touch was far too long. "I *am* an excellent seamstress."

"Indeed."

"But how do you know they aren't looking at you? You're quite handsome tonight as well."

"Nope, but thank you for the compliment. If you've seen one monkey suit, you've seen them all. Tonight is all about you. And you deserve it."

Cynthia was a little startled by his statement. She'd been lucky. She doubted she'd been spared because she deserved it more than anyone else on that plane. To be honest, she should've been one of the last ones spared. "For what? Not dying?"

"You're a fighter. I'm so amazed at how you've handled everything that has been thrown at you the past few months. I didn't realize you had it in you. I guess I never really gave you enough credit. I was always too busy to really see who you were, only what you wanted me and everyone else to see."

Will stopped turning and they both became still in each other's arms. He reached down and gently tipped her chin up to him so she couldn't avoid his gaze. "I see you now, Cynthia. And I really like what I see."

Cynthia was trapped in the blue eyes gazing down on her with adoration and unmasked attraction. It was the nicest thing he'd ever said to her. It wasn't a declaration of love, but it was a step in the right direction. She'd held on to the dream of a real future together, but she figured it would take time. When she gave him back the engagement ring, it was a pledge to put in the necessary time and effort to fix their relationship. Perhaps it wasn't as broken as she'd thought. They could have a future together. One filled with love and laughter.

As she stood there, surrounded by the gentle glow of crystal chandeliers and drifting orchestra music, she felt her heart slipping from her grasp. She barely knew Will, but she didn't care. She knew he was honest and kind. He supported her like no one else had. He'd protected her from a world that seemed to come at her from all sides. He was a good man. A man worthy of the love that suddenly swelled in her chest for him.

Cynthia really did love him. And she wanted to tell him how she felt in this perfect moment, but she knew it was too soon. The night had been an emotional roller coaster, but she knew how it needed to end. She needed to find the solace and comfort she knew would be in Will's arms. And in his bed.

Maybe there she could find the courage to voice the words that wanted to burst out of her with their intensity.

Instead she said, "Kiss me." And he did without hesitation.

She melted into him, neither of them worried about her makeup or the fact that a hundred people were watching them. It was just him and her, two lovers in a bubble that no one, not even Nigel, could burst.

When they finally came up for air, Cynthia knew she couldn't stay at this party a moment longer. She needed to make love to Will.

"Now, we've danced. So take me home," she demanded with a wicked smile.

Nine

Cynthia sat expectantly in the limousine, eyeing Will as though he would pounce on her at any moment, but he wasn't about to start anything he couldn't finish. She couldn't walk up to the apartment carrying her dress, and she'd kill him if he ripped it off her the way he wanted to, so there was nothing to do but wait.

A little anticipation never hurt anyone. The past few days had taught him that.

But Cynthia wasn't having it. She moved over to the opposite seat, facing him. Having her out of his reach was helpful, but now he couldn't keep from looking at her. Which is exactly what she wanted.

Grasping at the fabric, she slowly inched her dress up her legs until they were exposed to the knee. He could see the bare flash of her inner thigh as she slipped out of her heels and stretched one pale, delicate foot across the distance between them. Starting at his ankle, it slowly snaked up his leg, gently caressing him as it went.

He tensed as her foot moved higher, slinking across his inner thigh. Will was firm, ready and aching for her touch. Her green eyes shone with a naughty glint as they locked on his. The corners of her mouth curved up in a knowing smile as her toes met with the base of his shaft and agonizingly slid up the hard length.

Will groaned aloud, his hands curving into tight fists at his sides. Thank God the privacy partition was up in the limousine. He didn't want their driver to hear him, and he couldn't keep the growl in his throat from escaping as her foot moved up and down in a rhythm set to make him absolutely crazy.

He would not reach for her, he told himself. They were almost home. Getting out of the car and upstairs might be an issue for him with her tiny pink-painted toes driving him to distraction, but he could do it.

"Aww," Cynthia pouted as the limo pulled up outside their building. "I was just starting to have some fun."

Will sighed in relief as she pulled her dress down and slipped back into her shoes. Cynthia gathered her things and slipped out of the door, which was now open and waiting for them. They made it upstairs in record time, the door slamming shut behind Will just as he thought he might explode if he didn't touch her soon.

But she moved out of his reach.

Taking a few steps back until she was highlighted in the dark apartment by the glow of the overhead entryway light, she held out a hand to urge him to stay where he was. He flopped back against the door, untying his tie to keep from choking on it as he realized what she had in mind.

Reaching up to her neck, she unfastened her necklace, exposing the wide, creamy expanse of her chest and throat. She set it on the nearby table and followed it one by one with her earrings and bracelets.

With a sly grin, she turned until her back was to him, looking over her shoulder with a wink. Her fingers moved up to her hair, finding the combs and pins that held it in place and removing them, letting her dark brown tresses fall in silky curls around her shoulders.

Then her arms twisted behind her and found the fastener at the top of the zipper. Cynthia undid it and then grasped the metal tab and dragged it down. Inch by inch, she revealed skin, his heart racing in his chest with every second that ticked by.

The zipper stopped just at the base of her spine. His eager eyes took in everything, including the fact that he'd yet to see evidence of any undergarments beneath that dress. No bra definitely, and he was beginning to think she hadn't worn panties either.

"Holy hell," he whispered, his throat becoming dry as a desert. All night there had been nothing between them but the elegant green material.

Holding the dress to her chest, she turned back to face him, her arms pressed so tightly that her breasts threatened to burst out of the top of her gown. They were tinged a pink color with a blush like her neck and face. It made him smile knowing she was trying so hard for him even when it was slightly out of her comfort zone. He wanted to tell her not to be embarrassed, that she was doing a damn good job, but before he could, she met his gaze with her own and the gown slipped to the floor.

It pooled at her feet, proving he'd been correct earlier. She'd worn a dress and shoes tonight, nothing more. If she'd told him that earlier, they never would've made it to the party.

She stepped out of the puddle of fabric, her graceful, nude body on full display for the first time. The expression on her face was a mix of nerves and arousal. Cynthia was giving herself fully to him tonight. Before, darkness had cloaked her just as she'd held back, but now her rounded belly and hips beckoned to him. Her perky, full breasts reached out with tight peach nipples that reminded him of her lip gloss from earlier. He knew they would taste just as sweet.

His body urged him to quickly close the gap between them, but he held his ground. As much as he wanted her, he wasn't going to rush tonight. Pushing away from the door, he slipped out of his tuxedo jacket and tossed it onto the coat rack. Taking one slow step after the other toward her, he pulled his tie off and threw it on the floor and then started unbuttoning one onyx button after the other.

He stopped just short of her, his shirt undone to his waist. Cynthia boldly reached out to tug it out of his waistband, undoing the last button and reaching up to slip the shirt off his shoulders. Her hands followed the fabric down his arms, her palms caressing him down his biceps, elbows and forearms until the shirt fell to the floor.

Will let her hands continue to explore as they ran over the muscles of his chest, sliding across the ridges of his abdomen and returning to unfasten his belt.

Her fingers were about to slip inside his waistband when his hand caught her wrist. She gasped in surprise. "I want to touch you," she said, pouting until he leaned in and wiped the frown away with his mouth.

Cynthia pressed her naked body against him, and he released her wrist so she could wrap her arms around his neck. The firm peaks of her breasts dug into his chest, the globes flattening to him as she struggled to get closer.

Their tongues and lips and teeth danced frantically together as his hands moved over her body, unfettered by the inconvenience of her clothing.

She gasped against his lips as one hand cupped her breast, her hips surging forward to press her soft belly against his pulsating erection. He groaned, closing his eyes and riding the wave of sensation she brought on. Her mouth took advantage of his pause to slide down his jaw to his throat, pressing soft kisses against his fevered skin. To his surprise, she bit him at the juncture of his neck and shoulder, sending a shock of pleasure that pushed him near the edge as she soothed the wound with her silken tongue.

She'd certainly gained some confidence since their first night together after the accident, and it was undeniably sexy. In one swift movement, Will dipped down and scooped Cynthia into his arms. She cried out in surprise and then giggled and nuzzled at his neck as they moved down the hallway to the bedroom.

"How very Rhett Butler of you," she said as he kicked the door open, switched on the light and laid her down on the comforter.

Will took a step back to admire the sprawled-out beauty on his bed. She looked so free and open to him. He had been given such a gift, and it had taken him this long to truly appreciate it. This woman was everything that he wanted. Four months ago no one could've convinced him that he would be where he was right now—with Cynthia naked, willing and on display for him. That he would be bursting with arousal and emotions he'd never felt before.

She was so beautiful it made his heart swell with pride that she was his. So full of life and energy it made him want to share his life with her. To experience it as her partner. Her lover. Alex was right. Will was lost. Despite his best attempts, he'd allowed himself to fall in love. Hopelessly, desperately in love with a woman who made him happy to come home from work every day. Who made him want to live life, not just write about it in the newspaper.

In that very moment, he had to possess her, heart and soul, and couldn't wait another moment. Without delay, he slipped off the last of his clothes, his gaze never straying from the feast before him.

Cynthia watched him anxiously through hooded eyes as he undressed, but her expression changed when she caught sight of his erection jutting proudly toward her. Her moist lips parted softly, and then the look of pleasure washed over her flushed face. With a smile, she crooked her finger at him to join her at last on the bed.

He'd waited long enough, and he wasn't about to deny her request.

Cynthia held her breath in anticipation as Will crawled onto the bed and covered her with his muscled body. The warmth of his skin seared across her exposed flesh, and a chill ran down her spine from the pleasurable contrast. He hovered just over her, her aching nipples dragging across his chest, the firm length of his erection grazing her stomach.

So close and yet so far away. She reached out to touch him, but he pulled back, moving down her body to settle between her legs. His hands ran up her shins, his palms tickling her as they moved higher. He knelt down and followed his hands with his mouth, first planting a warm kiss on the inside of her ankles and then traveling up her calves to the insides of her knees.

Knees were hardly an erogenous zone, but Cynthia's whole body was tense and sensitive to his every caress. As he gently parted her thighs, he exposed her moist core and her legs started trembling. She couldn't stop it, her body so weak with wanting him as his kisses traveled over her inner thighs, his fingertips tracing lazy circles across her skin.

By the time she could feel his hot breath tickling her dark, feminine curls, she thought even his slightest touch might send her over the edge. Will explored her with his hand first, running along the edge with his finger before slowly slipping it inside of her. Her muscles clamped down around him, desperate to hold him there, but it wasn't what she wanted. She wanted him.

He leaned in and his tongue struck her sensitive center without fail, the intimate kiss sending waves of pleasure through her body. Cynthia squirmed under his touch, her hips rising up to meet him and then pulling away when the intensity became too much.

"I need you," she whispered.

"You'll have me," he said, his voice deep and gruff with arousal. "I want to have a little fun first."

This time she whimpered as his fingers and tongue pushed her closer to the edge. She didn't want to peak without him. She'd admitted to herself tonight that she loved him. She'd exposed herself to him in every way, made herself so vulnerable she almost couldn't believe it. She wanted her first cries of pleasure as a woman in love to be mingled with his own. "Not without you. Not tonight, Will."

Her pleas were finally heard, and he moved back up her body, nestling between her thighs and looking down at her. He reached to the nightstand for a condom, and Cynthia sighed in relief that he'd thought of it when she'd been too overwhelmed with desire to think straight.

A moment later, he hovered over her, the tip of him pressing gently at her entrance. Without hesitation, he drove into her, and then he lingered—buried deep inside her. It was a powerful feeling, to finally join with the man she loved. So much so she almost had to fight back tears that the connection brought on. The words she longed to say hung on the tip of her tongue, waiting to be uttered, but he started moving inside her, and the time for talking passed.

Will dropped his weight on to his elbows, pressing his chest against hers. He kissed her, his lips and tongue melding with her own as he gently rocked back and forth. Every inch of their bodies were touching and molding together. Cynthia could feel every flex of his muscles, every shudder of strain as he fought to hold back the tides. But she didn't want him to do that. She wanted all of him tonight, leaving nothing behind.

"Love me the way you want to. Don't hold back," she said against his jaw.

Will didn't answer but buried his face into her neck. His rapid breaths were hot again her skin, his body stiffening to surge forward harder and faster than before. The delicious movement accelerated every impulse running through her nervous system, the pleasurable sparks lighting up all over.

It wasn't long before the tight knot of tension in her belly threatened to explode. Cynthia wrapped her legs around his waist and clutched at his back. The change in angle allowed him to drive deeper, a low roar of pleasure echoing into her ear.

She couldn't hold back any longer. "Will!" she cried out, as one long, hard stroke sent her over the edge. Her body was racked with convulsions of pleasure, her muscles tightening and pulsating around his firm heat. Her fingertips dug into the muscles of his back, scrambling for purchase as he continued to pound deep inside. At last, his own release exploded, his groan of surrender vibrating against the damp skin of her neck.

For a few moments, they lay motionless, their bodies a moist tangle of limbs and sheets. Cynthia struggled to draw a full breath into her lungs, but she couldn't. Her muscles were too tired and her heart too swollen with unspoken emotions. By the time the last throbs of pleasure subsided, she opened her eyes to see Will looking down at her.

"You," he said, propping up on one elbow and brushing a damp strand of hair from her forehead, "were amazing tonight. You were so worried about fitting in with those people, but it was effortless. You were so elegant and graceful. Every woman in that ballroom wanted to wear your clothing and hoped they'd look half as good in them as you did.

"And all the men…" he continued. "Well, let's just say I got to live out their fantasies tonight."

"I got to live out my fantasy tonight, too."

Will smiled, leaning down to place a soft kiss on her lips.

Her body responded to his touch, but her brain chased the heat out of her veins. It was time to sleep, at least for now.

He reached down to pull the duvet up to cover them, and then tugged Cynthia up to curl her back against his chest. Wrapped in the warmth of the blanket with Will beside her, they fell asleep, the lights still on, their clothes still strewn around the apartment.

Sometime before dawn, Cynthia woke up, still tucked in Will's strong embrace. She squirmed slightly to free herself from his grasp and sat up on the edge of the bed.

"Are you all right?" he asked, his voice sleepy and rough.

"Yes," she said. "I'm just thirsty, and I never brushed my teeth. Do you want some water?"

"No, I'm okay."

Cynthia pushed up from the mattress and walked nude into the bathroom. At the doorway, she paused and looked back at Will. She expected to catch a glimpse of him as he fell back asleep, but he was propped up on his elbow. He was watching her walk away, but the expression on his face was not what she was expecting. His brow was furrowed, his gaze burrowing into her backside, of all places.

"Is something wrong?" she asked.

Will shifted his gaze to her, the intensity only increasing as he studied her face just as thoroughly. "No," he said pointedly, although his contemplative tone made her wonder if that were really true.

Cynthia was too sleepy to worry much about it. She went into the bathroom and shut the door behind her. She chugged a cup of water, finished removing her makeup and went about her nightly beauty regime. Her body was aching, but fulfilled, and she was eager to crawl back under the covers and sleep in Will's arms until noon.

Returning to the bed, she switched off the lights and slipped under the sheets. Will had rolled onto his back and his eyes were closed. She snuggled into him and laid her head on his chest. Listening to his heartbeat, she realized she'd never been so happy. Finding a passion in sewing and design was nothing compared to finding a passion and love for Will. Tonight had been everything she hoped and wished for when she gave him back her engagement ring—a chance for them to start over and be happy together.

"I love you," she whispered into the dark once the rise and fall of his breath became steady and even against her and she was certain he was sleeping. Then she turned onto her side and closed her eyes, immediately falling asleep.

Although he was lying in bed with his eyes closed, Will was far from asleep. Ten minutes ago, he would've told anyone he was exhausted and content with the woman he loved in his arms. His business was doing well and his love life was better than ever. Somehow, all of that was snatched from him so quickly that he couldn't feel the pain of it being ripped away at first. There was just a mix of confusion and denial swirling around the sleepy fog of his brain. What he'd just seen was impossible. Incomprehensible. And yet there was no way to deny the truth.

The rose tattoo was gone.

He'd hated that thing from the moment she'd gotten it. Cynthia had gone off on a spring break girls' trip to Cancun their senior year at Yale. Sometime amongst the sun and surf and tequila, she'd decided it would be a great idea to commemorate the trip with a tattoo on her ass.

It was pretty and well done, but in the end, it was a red rose inked into her left butt cheek. He'd done his best to ignore it over the years, and when their love life fizzled, he'd forgotten it was even there.

Until it wasn't.

When he watched her walk away, the realization hit him like an iron fist to the gut. There was no tattoo. And not even the faintest hint of where one might've been removed by a laser without his knowledge. There was nothing. He didn't know what to say when she asked if something was wrong.

Yes, by God, something was very wrong. She was not Cynthia Dempsey, and that was a problem.

In an instant, his entire world came crashing down around him. The best relationship he'd ever had was built on nothing but lies. He could feel it disintegrating around him. Everything she'd said and everything they'd done in the past few weeks meant absolutely nothing.

Who had he just made love to? This woman, this Cynthia imposter...who was she, and how had she ended up living another person's life? The doctors said she had amnesia. Did she even know she *wasn't* Cynthia? Was this all just one tragic mixup, or had this woman deliberately taken advantage of her circumstances? Was it possible that despite her outward appearance, she was as manipulative as Cynthia?

All this time he'd been afraid to let his guard down because he didn't think he could trust Cynthia not to hurt him again. But he took the leap and found there was a greater pain he hadn't felt yet. The woman he loved, the one who'd gotten under his skin and made him question the way he lived his life, wasn't Cynthia at all. Cynthia never had the power to hurt him this badly because he hadn't allowed it. This time he'd let down his protective walls and permitted his mystery lover to shatter his heart, whereas Cynthia had merely cracked it.

It took every ounce of strength he had to keep his jaw clamped shut and swallow the hurt, confused words in his throat when she snuggled into his chest, completely oblivious to his discovery. The woman in his arms was not Cynthia. It was nearly impossible to wrap his head around the idea. His mind bounced around frantically, reliving every discussion, every touch, trying to determine if it had been obvious but he'd been too blinded by her light to see it.

No wonder Cynthia had cheated on him. He'd been with

her since college but he barely knew her anymore. They'd become so disconnected from their relationship that he couldn't even tell her from someone else. He, of all people, should've been able to tell the difference regardless of what some plastic surgeon's knife had done. He was a fool.

Will wanted to shake her and start throwing angry accusations, but it was 3 a.m. and he knew the answers wouldn't come. In the morning he would uncover the truth and then see what she had to say for herself. For now, all he could do was try to fall back asleep and hope the heartburn-like pain in his chest didn't keep him up all night.

It was then, as he lay in the dark praying for sleep to dull the pain, that the woman lying in his bed quietly declared that she was in love with him. And to think, up until that point, he'd thought the situation couldn't get any worse.

Ten

When morning had finally come around, the arrival of the sun did not make Will's outlook any brighter. In fact, he'd lay there wide awake the entire time. With each second that ticked by, the pain and confusion had slowly morphed into anger and suspicion. He got out of bed around seven and told her there was a pressing problem with the Sunday edition. He couldn't very well tell her he didn't want to be around her, pretending to bask in their post lovemaking glow. He wasn't a very good actor, and he wasn't ready to confront her until he had all the information. He wanted to have the advantage, and that meant doing the necessary research to figure out who she was and what she was after.

She—*he couldn't think of her as Cynthia anymore*—pouted appropriately and gave him a kiss to help keep her on his mind all day.

Oh, yeah, she'd be on his mind, all right. But probably not the way she imagined.

When he got to the office, he asked his weekend admin

to pull any articles the local papers had done on the plane crash. He spent two hours at his desk poring over the pieces published in his paper and other papers around town. There wasn't much information aside from details of the accident itself, the short list of survivors and what the airline was doing to ensure the tragedy would never happen again.

None of that was helpful.

Going down the hallway into the bullpen, where a large group of journalists worked in cubicles, he sought out the guy who had written all the articles for the *Observer*.

"Mike? Do you have a second?"

The journalist spun in his chair, a look of surprise on his face when he realized the owner of the paper was in his cubicle and not the guy across from him looking to borrow a stapler. "Yes, Mr. Taylor?"

"I'm looking for some information on Cynthia's plane crash. Do you happen to have any research materials left over that I can see?"

"Sure thing." Mike spun back around to his file cabinet and pulled out a green file labeled "Chicago Flight 746." "Everything I have is here, including any official faxes the airline sent."

"Is there a list of passengers and seats included?"

"Yes, sir."

"Excellent. Thank you, Mike."

Will took the file back to his office and flipped through the pages. According to the information from the airline, Cynthia was in 14A, a window seat in coach. That was unusual. A look at the first-class passengers explained it. Looked like a large group of Japanese businessmen traveling together. She probably hadn't realized what seat she was assigned until it was too late to change it.

Turning back to Cynthia's row, he noted the person beside her in 14B was a woman named Adrienne Lockhart. She had not survived the accident. Few had.

Firing up his laptop, Will pulled up his internet browser and searched for this Adrienne Lockhart. The first link was adriennelockhartdesigns.com, a site for a SoHo-based fashion designer.

A fashion designer. Will's stomach started to churn with dread. He was certainly on the right track. He'd hoped for a moment he'd find she'd sat beside a middle-aged attorney named Harold.

He opened the website up and saw on the homepage an announcement that the store was closing and thanking her patrons for their support. The announcement was dated the day before the crash.

Will clicked on "About the Designer," and before the page had almost fully loaded, he knew he had come to the right site. There was a photo of a smiling, dark-haired woman posted there. They could've been sisters with like features arranged in a slightly different way. She looked to be a similar build to Cynthia, but facially, there were differences. Adrienne's face was a touch rounder, her nose slightly wider. She didn't have Cynthia's high, prominent cheekbones or expensive, perfect teeth. Her hair had a sort of wavy kink to it, although it was the same dark color.

Clicking on the picture, it enlarged and he was able to zoom in on the feature he was most interested in. The eyes. He'd convinced himself that the gold in Cynthia's eyes had always been there, but he'd avoided her gaze so long he'd forgotten. Now he realized it was because it hadn't been there before. But it was certainly in this photo. If he enlarged the picture enough to show nothing else but the pair of green-gold eyes, it was like looking at Cynthia.

The Cynthia he'd made the mistake of falling for.

Cynthia Dempsey was not in his apartment. That woman was most certainly Adrienne Lockhart.

But why? How had this happened?

There had obviously been some kind of mistake at the accident site. Either the bodies had been thrown from their seats or they'd switched seats for some reason. He knew Cynthia hated the window, so he had no doubt she would needle the person next to her into trading. As badly as they were hurt, the women looked similar enough to be confused by rescue crews.

If Adrienne had woken up in the hospital, her face reconstructed to look more like Cynthia…it was an easy mistake for everyone to make. She had looked horrible, nothing like Cynthia at first despite Dr. Takashi's best efforts. They believed she was Cynthia because the doctors told them she was. But it was also an easy mistake to correct. All she had to do was say, "I'm not Cynthia Dempsey" the minute she could talk. But she hadn't. She'd feigned confusion and was diagnosed with amnesia.

Well, of course it would seem like it. She wouldn't recognize any of the people that came to see her. They'd never met. She wouldn't recognize their house or know anything about their life or her past. It made perfect sense.

Except she hadn't remembered who she really was either.

He'd always believed amnesia was the stuff of soap operas before Cynthia's accident. And now, knowing the truth, he was inclined to believe it still was.

The woman on that website was at the end of her rope. She'd lost her store, was flying back home to Wisconsin. She had nothing when she got on that plane. Even if there had been some initial confusion when she woke up with all the surgeries and drugs, there had to be a point when she realized there was a mistake and didn't say anything.

But why? Did the fancy life Cynthia no longer needed seem more glamorous? Rich parents, a penthouse apartment on the Upper East Side, a five-carat platinum engagement ring…certainly better than returning home a failure.

Better to go along with it, see how long she could get away with her game. In a matter of weeks, she'd overtaken Cynthia's life and set it on the course of the life she wanted. Not only was she designing, and miraculously well for a supposed novice, but now she had all the industry connections to get a collection off the ground.

It was certainly a big risk to take. She couldn't have known about the tattoo, but there could've been a million different ways to give her game away. Seducing him was probably the stupidest thing she could've done. Did she think he would be blinded by love and never notice the differences?

It had worked pretty well, so far. He'd dismissed the shoes being too big and the eyes being too gold. Cast aside doubts when she was suddenly a world-class seamstress. Suppressed his amazement when the personalities were like night and day. He supposed he had been blind. He hadn't wanted to see that no bump to the head could've turned the cold, indifferent woman he knew into the vivacious, loving woman who had charmed him from the first day in the hospital.

But perhaps that was all an act. If she were shrewd enough to steal another person's identity, all of that could just be part of the game. Be sweet, be loving, be innocent and everyone would love her too much to ask questions.

Slamming his fist into his desk, Will let himself focus on the pain radiating up his arm. The unpleasant sensation was the only thing in his life he knew was real and true. Cynthia or Adrienne or whoever the hell she was had wrapped him in such a web of lies that he didn't know what to believe. But pain didn't lie. It didn't turn your whole world upside down and confess its love to you in a ploy to hijack someone's life.

Well, no more. He wasn't about to be used for a second longer. He shut down his laptop and grabbed his coat off the back of his chair, then he marched out of his office to hail a cab for home.

Sunday afternoon Cynthia was filled with nervous energy. She should've been floating around on cloud nine after the amazing night she shared with Will, but something about this morning hadn't sat right with her. He'd come so far in his attempt to work less and spend more time with her. But this morning, he had almost avoided her. He didn't make eye contact. His lips had been stiff against hers when she kissed him goodbye. Then he'd dashed out the door to go to the office for a problem that someone other than the CEO could have fixed.

It made her uneasy. She thought last night had gone so well. She didn't know what the problem could be. Unless he heard her when she'd said she loved him. Cynthia had been certain he was asleep, but what if he wasn't? What if it was way too soon? She was a fool. *Always wait for the guy to say it first.*

As time went by without word from Will, Cynthia opted to call Darlene Winters. She should've waited until Monday, but she needed the distraction. She was pleased to find the fashion editor was still just as excited to view her work. She was to bring three pieces and her sketches to her office in the *Trend Now* magazine headquarters on Tuesday.

The problem was she only had three completed pieces: the gown, the shirt-dress and a coordinating skirt and blouse. If she took those three pieces, she didn't have the option of wearing one of her own designs. She didn't think any of her sketches could be completed in time, because she was short on the fabrics and supplies she would need. She'd just have to settle for the small fortune of designer clothes she owned.

She stood in her closet, eyeing the endless racks of items to wear. Cynthia had already picked out a deep purple skirt. She liked the pop of color, and the lines were similar enough to her collection that the style didn't contrast too much with what she promoted. But she still needed a blouse.

She flipped through hanger after hanger, the dollar signs adding up exponentially, but nothing caught her eye. Then she saw a glimpse of fabric in her peripheral vision. The flash of purple and white drew her down several feet to a long-sleeved blouse. She pulled it off the rack and looked it over. It was perfect, really. The purple and white stripes would accent the skirt, and some of the details in the blouse were very similar to what she'd been thinking about using in her own collection. Curious, she glanced at the tag on the collar.

Adrienne Lockhart Designs.

She looked at the name, staring intently at it for several moments as her brain tried to process the sudden influx of information rushing forward at once. It was like a dam had broken. Every memory she'd ever had bombarded her.

She remembered designing and sewing this blouse. The woman who bought it at her boutique was looking for a unique birthday gift. Her friend was the kind of person who had everything and she'd been struggling to find something different. Adrienne had hoped the woman would bring in more business, but nothing had ever come of it.

She could now picture her funky little shop with walls lined with clothing she'd designed and sewn herself. The fortune in her father's life insurance money she'd used to get started. The heartache of packing everything up to ship home to Wisconsin when it didn't work out.

Adrienne Lockhart.

The hanger slipped from her fingers to the floor, but she didn't bother to bend over and pick it up.

"My name is Adrienne Lockhart." She said the words aloud to the empty closet, and for the first time in two months, the niggling sensation in the back of her mind wasn't there. The name Cynthia Dempsey had always triggered a feeling that things weren't right. And they weren't.

Because Cynthia Dempsey was dead and buried in Wisconsin with a tombstone that had Adrienne's name on it.

A rush of emotion and confusion washed over her. She'd been living a lie for months. Fell in love with a dead woman's fiancé. Made love to him several times, all the while he believed she was someone else. How could she tell him the truth? What would he do?

He'd said he liked her better now than before, but would the fact that she wasn't Cynthia Dempsey change how he felt?

Never once when she thought about when and how she would regain her memory did it ever occur to her that she would realize she was someone else. Everyone thought she was dead. Cynthia's family thought she was alive. All of Cynthia's friends, the people who'd come to her party last night, pleased to see she was doing so well…how could she tell them the truth? How could she explain any of this?

Nausea swept over her. Rushing from the closet, she raced into the bathroom and lost her lunch in the fancy porcelain toilet.

Why hadn't she gone with her instincts? Alarm bells had been sounding the entire time to warn her that this life wasn't hers. She never had money or expensive anything. She was convinced that her tiny apartment in New York was an old janitorial closet. Her house in Milwaukee was a small, three-bedroom cottage in the suburbs that she inherited when her father died. The nicest piece of jewelry she owned was the strand of pearls that belonged to her mother. They were irreplaceable, but even then, they couldn't touch the value of Cynthia's jewels.

Rolling back against the wall, she wiped her mouth and was relieved that the engagement ring wasn't on her hand. It belonged to a woman from an entirely different world. That woman had been a successful advertising executive. That woman had clothes and credit card limits that Adrienne could only dream of. She was also a horrible person who cheated on her fiancé and made a mess of her own life.

Her one moment of relief was knowing she'd never actually done those terrible things. Nigel was a complete stranger. Along with everyone else, including Will.

Oh, God, Will.

Adrienne buried her face in her hands. This was such a mess. "How am I going to tell him?" she said aloud.

"How are you going to tell me *what?*"

Adrienne's head snapped up and found Will standing in the doorway of the bathroom. Things had apparently gone well at the paper. Not so much back here.

She immediately noticed a change in him. There was no softness in his eyes. His cold gaze was focused on her like a laser. His hands were thrust angrily in his pockets, his entire body tense from the chiseled line of his jaw to the wide, solid stance in the doorway.

"I…" she began, but couldn't find the words. What would she say? *My memory has suddenly come back, and I realized I'm not your fiancée. Sorry I slept with you.* Something like that?

"Why don't you do us both a favor and just come clean, *Adrienne?*"

Her eyes widened, her mouth falling open at once. He knew. Somehow he'd managed to piece it all together before she did. "I just remembered—"

"No way. Don't you even try to feed me some half-ass cover story about how you've just suddenly regained your memory because I've caught you."

"Caught me?" Adrienne's heart sank in her chest. She'd been worried enough that he'd be disappointed to find out she wasn't Cynthia but had hoped he'd understand the mistake. That perhaps their feelings for one another would overcome the reality of who she really was. But her hopes had been quickly dashed by the heated tone of his accusations. Apparently he was angry. And he somehow believed she'd faked everything for nefarious reasons.

"What a sweet stroke of luck it must've been for you. A failed business, no friends, no family, no money. Get on a plane and wake up a millionaire heiress with a new face making you the center of attention."

Adrienne climbed to her feet, tears she didn't want gathering in her eyes. "No," she insisted. "It isn't like that. I had no idea—"

"And to think I believed you'd uncovered a hidden talent, like some prodigy of the fashion world. Was it your plan all along to show your work to Darlene? Were you just using Cynthia's connections to further your career?"

"Why would I do that?" she asked. "It wouldn't be my career. It would be Cynthia's. This whole life was Cynthia's, and I knew I never fit into it. But everyone kept telling me this was who I was and that eventually I would remember."

"It's hard to remember a life you never lived."

The angry edge of Will's voice sent the tears spilling down her cheeks. She couldn't fight them anymore. "How did you find out?"

"You never should've seduced me, Adrienne. Dr. Takashi didn't work on anything but your face. It was a big risk to take off all your clothes and hope you looked the same from head to toe."

Adrienne flinched as her ego took the hit. Of course she never would've done that if she'd known the truth. Cynthia was perfect and thin and elegant. She was none of those things, and naked, it would be even more obvious. But she had to ask. "What was it about me that convinced you I wasn't her?"

"Cynthia had a rose tattoo. You don't."

Tattoo? That explained the odd look on his face as she walked to the bathroom last night. The way he'd stared intently at her rear end like the secrets of the universe were etched there. He was looking for a tattoo she didn't have. Their prior encounter had been dark, but that night the lights had been on while they made love and when she'd gotten out of bed. He'd known in that moment and she'd been stupid enough to turn around and tell him she loved him not twenty minutes later.

"Of course I don't. I'm afraid of needles. I would never have the nerve to get a tattoo."

"But you have the nerve to take advantage of a family that should be grieving the loss of their daughter?"

How could he think she would do that? Hadn't he learned anything about her in the past few weeks? "I didn't know. I swear I didn't know. Not until just now. In the closet I found a shirt—"

"The closet!" Will sneered, refusing to let her finish a complete thought. He obviously didn't care to hear anything she had to say in her defense. "I should've known the very first day you came home. Didn't know your own mother, but you knew when you'd landed the couture clothing jackpot. I bet you couldn't wait to see if you and Cynthia wore the same size."

"No," she insisted. "It was all real. Everything I said or did. I gave my heart to you, Will. I never would've done that if this was all a lie. I would never deliberately hurt you like *she* did."

A mottled red spread across Will's face, his nostrils flaring to indicate she'd said the wrong thing. "Don't you dare turn this on Cynthia. She may not have been perfect, but she never pretended to be anything she wasn't."

"Except in love with you." Adrienne couldn't help but shoot the sharp barb back at him in anger. "She probably never cared half as much for you as I do. She was in love with a broke artist from the Bronx. She was only using you as a cover so all her society friends wouldn't know she'd stoop that low."

Will shook his head slowly, the anger seeming to finish running its course, leaving him disillusioned and sad. "I never thought the woman I'd come to know the past few weeks would stoop this low either."

Adrienne tried to think of the right words for the moment.

The thing to convince him she meant everything she said. There was only one thing left. "I love you, Will."

"Get out."

Panic seized Adrienne, her chest tightening so suddenly she almost couldn't breathe. That wasn't the reaction she was hoping for. *Get out?* He couldn't really mean it. He wasn't cruel enough to throw her out with nothing. She didn't have a dime to her name. No cell phone, not even a driver's license. Everything she owned was Cynthia's. Adrienne had lost all her possessions in the crash. Even if she somehow managed to have her aunt wire her money, could she buy a bus ticket without ID? How was she going to get home?

"Will, please," she begged. She had to persuade him to see reason.

"I said get out!" he yelled, his voice booming in the acoustic bathroom.

In that moment, Adrienne knew the battle was over. There was no way she could convince him of the truth. Nodding, she started for the exit to the bathroom, waiting for him to step aside so she could get through the doorway.

"You think you know what happened. You think I'm a horrible person. I can't change that. But I meant what I said. I did fall in love with you."

He stepped aside to let her by but turned his face away, unwilling to look at her for the sincerity or truth of her words. He obviously didn't want to hear anything she had to say. Will had made his decision, delivered his verdict and executed the sentence. As far as he was concerned, Adrienne was as dead as everyone thought she was.

Defeated, Adrienne walked down the hallway, through the living room and out of his life.

't like. "There's nothing to talk about, because
ia Dempsey."

t your new story?" Nigel sneered at her, his
ng with irritation. "And who are you now, Miss
hty?"

o one believe her when she tried to tell the truth?
mixup at the hospital. My name is Adrienne.
I was Cynthia, but I've regained my memory
w that I'm not."

wned at her. "Do you really think I'm that

d she prove it to him? Maybe the same way she'd
y convinced Will. "I have no rose tattoo, Nigel.
would've seen it at some point. I'm not going to
ts in the street, but you can believe me when I
hrew me out of the apartment because the tattoo
. That's why I'm wandering around Manhattan
at, a purse or a dime to my name."

uggled to swallow a hard lump in his throat. "If
enne, then where the hell is Cynthia?"

squeezed her eyes shut. Every time she thought
dn't get worse, fate slapped her down and proved
Did she really have to connect those dots for him?
t have him stalking her around town when she
e safe to go, so she supposed she had to. "I'm
you this, but Cynthia was killed in the plane
confused us and thought I was dead instead of

ne had thought he was angry before, she was
el's jaw locked, his face flushing crimson with
lying to me!" He lunged toward her, and his
efore she could react. His fist made contact with
ding her flying backward.

thing she remembered was the cold sensation of

Eleven

Adrienne stood outside the storefront that had once been
her boutique. Her funky little shop had a banner across
the window announcing the grand opening of a new Baby
GAP. She could see the overpriced clothes for baby yuppies
hanging where her beautiful, artistic creations once were.
She wanted to cry. To scream and throw a rock through the
window.

It was bad enough when she'd lost her shop. Not everyone had the talent to make it, and she was mature enough to
understand that. But now she knew she did have the talent.
With the right connections, Cynthia's network could've
launched her career. Even if it had been as Cynthia Dempsey,
it would've been fulfilling her dreams. And once again, she'd
lost her chance.

Just like she'd lost her chance with Will. And that was
even worse than her latest discovery.

She'd give up designing clothes to have the chance to make
things right with him. He'd probably never forgive her or

trust her again, but she wished he'd give her the opportunity to try. She'd never get it, though. Just like when he discovered Cynthia was cheating, he cut Adrienne from his life with one clean swipe. He was through. And even if he had second thoughts, they would come too late. Adrienne would be back in Milwaukee before long, working retail or finding some part-time job as a seamstress altering wedding dresses.

Somehow things were better when she was dead.

She clutched her arms to her chest, the cool breeze raising goose bumps across her bare flesh. She'd dressed for a lazy Sunday at home—a pair of comfy jeans, a cotton T-shirt and sneakers. She should've grabbed a coat before she left the apartment, but she didn't want Will to accuse her of stealing Cynthia's clothes. As it was, she was surprised he didn't force her out of the apartment naked.

It didn't really matter, though. No amount of cold air could distract her from the pain of the gaping hole in her chest. She thought she'd lost everything when the plane crashed, but she was wrong. What she'd lost since then was much worse. The man she loved hated her. The people she thought of as her family would, too, once they knew the truth. Adrienne didn't know what to do.

She'd wandered aimlessly through the streets with no real destination in mind and found herself in her old stomping grounds in SoHo. She didn't really know where else she could go. Hours had gone by and the sun was about to set, making her situation more serious by the minute. Her best option would be to see if she could crash at Gwen's place until she could get the money to go home, but she didn't have her phone number on her. Adrienne's only other choices were to show up unannounced at one of her old friends' places and give them a huge shock, since they thought she was dead, or find a homeless shelter.

From the penthouse to a semiprivate cot in just a few hours' time. It was such a disaster. And to think she'd woken

up believing the world was [...] love, her career was taking o[...] worry about her persistent am[...] for her.

Well, standing on the side[...] helping anything. She headed [...] she could find Gwen and pray[...] Adrienne was about to turn th[...] Village when she felt an iron ha[...]

Just great.

Homeless, penniless, hopele[...] going to mug her. And take wha[...] pride, and that wouldn't go for m[...] Spinning on her heel, ready to fen[...] she found herself face-to-face wit[...]

"What are you doing?" she sc[...] hell out of me." Adrienne jerked fr[...] backward.

Nigel looked like hell. He hadi[...] shaved since she saw him at the p[...] to believe he hadn't slept either. [...] wrinkled, his eyes bloodshot and w[...] deprivation. He looked like a man[...]

"How did you find me here? D[...] Nigel nodded. "I've been watch[...] you leave. I followed you to try and[...]

"You've been following me aro[...] A deep sense of unease was pooli[...] stomach. The last words he'd sp[...] and then he'd started stalking her. [...] back. If he had a weapon, she did[...] ing range.

"I did what I had to do. I need[...] There was a growing edge of[...]

Adrienne did[...]
I'm not Cynt[...]
"Oh, is th[...]
upper lip cur[...]
High and Mi[...]
Why did [...]
"There was [...]
They though[...]
and know n[...]
Nigel fr[...]
stupid?"
How cou[...]
unknowing[...]
I know you[...]
drop my p[...]
say it. Will[...]
was missing[...]
without a c[...]
Nigel st[...]
you're Adr[...]
Adrienn[...]
her life cou[...]
her wrong. [...]
She couldn[...]
had no plac[...]
sorry to tel[...]
crash. They[...]
her."
If Adrie[...]
wrong. Nig[...]
anger. "Sto[...]
hand flew [...]
her chin, s[...]
The last[...]

the concrete sidewalk against her back and the loud thunk of her head as it hit the ground and knocked her out.

"I don't understand. What was she doing in SoHo without any money or identification? Was she mugged?"

Adrienne recognized the voice of Pauline Dempsey, her tone growing more shrill with concern. For a minute, everything was jumbled in her mind. Where was she? The last thing she remembered was fighting with Nigel. How did she end up in a room with Cynthia's parents? She was curious but didn't want to open her eyes. Her head hurt too much, and she was sure the lights illuminating her eyelids wouldn't help.

"It's possible, but I doubt it. The cops seem to think she was assaulted by someone she knew. The 911 dispatcher said the male caller gave her name. Without ID, no one would've known who she was otherwise."

"I bet it was that man from last night. I knew I should've called security. How is my little girl going to get better at this rate?" This time the voice was her father's. Or rather, George Dempsey's.

Was she in the hospital again? Wait…Nigel hit her when she told him Cynthia was dead. She must've been knocked pretty hard to black out.

"She's going to be fine. Fortunately, the man who hit her struck her jaw and not her cheekbones or any of the other parts that are still healing from surgery. She has a concussion, so we'll need to keep an eye on her for a little bit, but I don't think it's very serious."

"Very serious?" George's voice grew louder with irritation. "My daughter can't remember who she is, and you think another blow to the head isn't serious?"

There was no way Adrienne was going to be able to stay floating around in the dark sea that comforted her. Someone had to put a stop to this circus. She forced her eyes open, her hand coming up quick to cup her jaw when a groan sent a bolt of pain through her face. "Ow."

"Cynthia?"

They still thought she was Cynthia. Will hadn't told them the truth. She had the opportunity to end things differently than she had with Will, and she wanted to. She didn't want the couple that had been so kind to her to hate her the way he did.

Adrienne pushed herself up and looked around. She was in a hospital bed again, one very similar to the one she'd woken up in a few weeks ago, if not the very same. Pauline and George were standing to her left, the doctor to her right. And in the back of the room, leaning against the wall, was Will.

He didn't say anything when she looked at him. He just watched her with cold indifference. He hated her; she could tell as much from the stiff crossing of his arms and hardened jaw. But he hadn't told Cynthia's parents the truth. Why? He'd seemed angry enough to want to expose her to everyone, and yet he hadn't.

"Cynthia, are you okay? What happened to you? Were you attacked?" Pauline was at her side in an instant, rubbing her arm protectively.

Adrienne shifted her gaze from Will and turned to the woman seated beside her.

"I'm not Cynthia," she said as she softly shook her head.

Pauline and George both frowned and looked at one another with concern. "What's that dear?" Pauline asked.

"My name isn't Cynthia. I remember now. I remember everything. My name's Adrienne. Adrienne Lockhart."

Her two former parents turned from her to the doctor, their eyes wide with confusion and concern.

"Doctor, what's going on?" George demanded.

The doctor frowned and approached the bed. He pulled out a pen light and shined it in her eyes while asking her questions about dates and political figures. She got all the answers right, but that didn't seem to make him any happier. "You say you're not Cynthia Dempsey?"

"Yes," she said, nodding her head and wincing with the movement. That bastard had hit her hard. "I'm certain my name is Adrienne. I'm from Milwaukee. My parents were Allen and Miriam Lockhart." She looked at Pauline and then George. "I don't understand how this could happen. How could I be confused with another person?"

Pauline pulled away, taking a few steps back to cradle herself against George's side. Adrienne hated to see the pained expressions on their faces. She didn't have to tell them the implications of her announcement like she had with Nigel. Only a small child and a teenage boy survived the crash with her. If she wasn't Cynthia, then their daughter was amongst the casualties.

"Your accident was very severe, and you were almost unrecognizable." The doctor was already covering his bases for the inevitable lawsuit. "Do you remember living as Cynthia?"

Adrienne nodded again. "I do. I don't recall the day of the accident, but I remember everything else, before and after the crash."

"It appears as though your memory loss has been reversed, perhaps by the second blow to the head. And that leads us to another unfortunate complication. Please excuse us," the doctor said to her. "I need to speak with the Dempseys in private." He held out his hand and ushered the couple into the hallway for more damage control.

Adrienne took a deep breath and flopped back against her pillows once the door shut. She closed her eyes as tears formed and blurred her vision of the angry man across from her bed. She refused to cry again with Will still there, watching her. He'd never believe the truth—that her heart was broken—and would probably accuse her of crocodile tears for sympathy.

"You didn't tell them," she said at last when he continued to stand there without speaking.

"I wanted to see if you did the right thing first."

She opened her eyes and looked at him. It was so hard to look at the man she loved and see the naked rage of a stranger instead. He was nothing like the relaxed, happy Will who had kissed her in Times Square and swept her across the dance floor at her party. All that was left was the cold, hard shell of a businessman poised to take down a competitor. There was no reading him. It made it impossible to know if she'd passed his test. "And?"

"And you're a better actress than I thought." At that, he turned and strode from the room without glancing back.

With the slam of the hospital room door, the last remaining fragments of love and hope left in Adrienne's heart shattered, and she could no longer hold back the tears.

"You can stay with me as long as you need to. Or can stand to. My apartment is a fifth-floor walkup and only four hundred square feet, so I expect you to be gone by Wednesday."

Gwen held out a key and a slip of paper with her address. "You just make yourself at home. Eat whatever you like. You can probably fit in some of my clothes, too, although the pants might run a little short on you since I come from a family of elves. I'll be home around six in the morning."

Adrienne leaned in and hugged Gwen fiercely. When it was all said and done, the only friend she'd made since her accident was the only one she had left. It had been less than twenty four hours since the news of Cynthia's death, and already the world had lost interest in Adrienne Lockhart.

"You don't know how much I appreciate this," Adrienne said, fighting the tears that were a constant threat of late.

"Not a problem, honey. Now, keep an eye on your jaw and that lump of yours. It's a good excuse to have a milkshake for dinner. I'll check on you in the morning to make sure you don't need to see the doctor again."

After being discharged Monday afternoon, Adrienne had gone to meet Gwen. Her plans were to go to her apartment, surprise her aunt with the news of her miraculous resurrection and ask her to wire some money to her. From there, she could buy a change of clothes and hopefully get a bus ticket. Trains were too expensive, and planes were out of the question.

She waved to Gwen and headed for the elevator. When she walked out of the hospital, she stopped short as a black town car pulled directly in front of her. The window rolled down in the back, and she was surprised to find Pauline Dempsey looking out at her.

"Mrs. Dempsey?"

"Pauline, dear, please. Do you have a ride to wherever you're going?"

The answer was no. Gwen had given her ten bucks for the subway and a strawberry milkshake. "I was going to take the subway."

The older woman looked appalled. "Absolutely not. You're a magnet for trouble, my dear. You'll get mugged again."

The door of the town car flew open and Adrienne had to leap back to keep from getting hit. "Are you sure?" She wasn't entirely comfortable around Cynthia's family now. Things had to be awkward for everyone.

"Get in the car, please."

Adrienne did as she was told, the authoritative and motherly tone leaving no question. She imagined it was hard for Pauline to look at her and not see her daughter. To not want to treat her the way she treated Cynthia.

Once inside, she shut the door and found Pauline was alone. "Do you have an address to give Henry?"

Adrienne passed the slip of paper over the seat to the driver and the car pulled away from the hospital.

"I called to find out what time you were being discharged. I wanted to talk to you before you went home to Wisconsin."

"Talk to me about what? I told the doctors I don't remember much." Adrienne had hoped her memory of the day of the accident and meeting Cynthia would return, but it continued to be a black hole. She figured it was probably better that way if she was ever going to get on a plane again.

"Dear, I'm not fishing for information. I'm concerned for you. Whether or not you are my daughter, I sat in that hospital every day for five weeks drinking bad coffee and praying for you to recover. I was so proud of you Saturday night at your party. You are a beautiful, talented young woman, and your parentage doesn't change that."

"Thank you." She was mildly uncomfortable with the woman's compliments. "I'm very sorry about Cynthia."

The older woman nodded and looked down at the hands folded in her lap. "I loved my oldest daughter very much, but she could be very difficult sometimes. There were days I thought Will was a saint to even tolerate her, much less marry her.

"But these past few weeks with you have been so nice. Even through the tears and anxiety of the accident, you were always such a sweet person. I should've known then you weren't my daughter, but I hoped she'd made a change for the better. I think maybe I'll keep those memories as my last memories of Cynthia. End our relationship on a more positive note."

Adrienne nodded but took a moment to figure out how to respond. "My mother died in a car accident when I was eight. She loved to sew, and I spent hours watching her make dresses and play clothes for me and my dolls. After her accident, I climbed up to her sewing machine and continued her work. That's where I got my passion for designing clothes.

"But I've always had a hole in my life where she was concerned. It's hard for a teenage girl to grow up with a single father. They don't understand anything. And when he died a few years ago, I had nothing left.

"If not for the mixup, I would've woken up in the hospital completely alone and spent the weeks of my recovery without anyone who cared. Even though you aren't really my parents, having you and George there for me these few short months has been priceless. I missed having family so much. I know speaking to me might be difficult for you both, but please feel free to keep in touch."

Adrienne could see the tears in Pauline's eyes even in the dark cabin of the car. "Thank you," she said, leaning forward and hugging Adrienne. "I would love to keep in touch and see how you are doing, how your career is going."

"I'm not sure I have much of a career left, but thanks for your vote of confidence. Actually, I don't have much of anything left. It feels sort of odd to think of it that way, but it's true. Everything I had was Cynthia's."

"I didn't think about that. You lost it all in the crash, didn't you? How terrible. How are you getting home?"

"I'm going to have my aunt wire me money for a bus ticket. Given I've been declared dead, she's the only one with access to my accounts."

Pauline's hand reached out to rest on Adrienne's knee. "I want to do something for you."

Surprised, Adrienne turned to the older woman and shook her head. "No, you've done enough for me. That party had to cost you a fortune."

"Nonsense. I want to help you get home, and I won't take no for an answer. If you insist on the bus, so be it, but the train runs from Penn Station to Chicago and up to Milwaukee. I figure you're probably not interested in flying, but if you'll let me, I'd like to buy a ticket for you."

"I can't accept that. I feel like I've already taken advantage of everyone in Cynthia's life. I wouldn't feel right taking anything else."

Pauline turned to her purse, reached inside and pulled out her cell phone. Before Adrienne could argue, she purchased a one-way ticket in a roomette for departure the following day. After she hung up, she looked at Adrienne with a smile. "The ticket will be waiting for you at the ticket counter tomorrow. The train departs at three forty-five in the afternoon."

"That's really not necessary."

"I do what I want to, dear."

She certainly couldn't argue with that and frankly didn't want to despite her protests. Three days of buses and sleeping in terminals was not her ideal trip. "Thank you. For everything."

"You brought light into all our lives. Even Will's. I know he's taken all this pretty hard. I'm sorry if he's been a little standoffish. But he was happier with you these past few weeks than I'd seen him in years. Watching you two dance at the party, I was certain he was in love with you. I'll be the first to admit you were a better match for him than my daughter. Maybe once the shock wears off, he'll realize he loves you the person, not the name."

Adrienne tried to look embarrassed by her words, but inside she was really fighting back tears. She didn't dare leave herself the hope of Will changing his mind. How could this woman understand the situation so completely when Will, the man she loved, adamantly refused? His stubborn, suspicious streak had cost them a chance at real happiness.

The car pulled up to the curb and Henry got out to open the door for Adrienne.

"Call us when you get home safely. I expect to hear from you at least once a month so I know you're not in some kind of trouble. That was my rule with Cynthia, and now it's my rule with you."

Adrienne hugged the woman again. "Yes, ma'am," she said before slipping out of the car. She stood on the curb and watched the town car merge back into traffic and disappear down the block.

She was a little sad watching Pauline drive away but was glad to know they'd keep in touch. If she couldn't have the man she loved, at least a relationship with Pauline and George was more than she had before the accident.

Slipping the key from her pocket, she unlocked the door and headed up the four flights of stairs to Gwen's apartment.

Twelve

Adrienne's homecoming to Wisconsin was not nearly as grand as her party in New York. Frankly, it was depressing, but it was a reflection of her life and the turn it had taken. Her aunt Margaret picked her up at the train station. They had never been very close; Aunt Margaret hadn't liked Adrienne's mother, so of course Miriam's daughter was tainted as well.

When Adrienne came out of the train station, Margaret was waiting in the snow with her station wagon, a frown drawing deep wrinkles into her face. Just as when she'd called on Monday, there were no tears of joy to see her alive again. Not even a hug. Only a complaint about the traffic and that Adrienne's train had arrived at rush hour.

All the way home, Margaret talked about the hassle and expense of arranging her funeral. Adrienne figured she was mostly irritated because she'd gone to all that trouble for a person whose death gained her nothing.

As they pulled up to her house, she saw Margaret look at the place with a touch of disgust in her eyes. Adrienne had seen the muddy, uprooted For Sale sign in the back of the wagon when she got in. Margaret's mood was probably tainted by the fact that she wouldn't get to move into Adrienne's house now that she was miraculously alive. She'd always eyed the place with envy when Adrienne's father was alive and had pressed Adrienne to sell it to her after he died. She'd probably put her own place up for sale and started planning her housewarming party before she'd begun the funeral arrangements.

Fortunately, Adrienne had never bowed to her aunt's pressure. She'd kept it and had a place to come back to. It was the only home she'd ever known. Her tiny apartment in New York hadn't qualified. The penthouse with Will had never felt right to her. Only this place, with her childhood memories of her parents, could put her at ease.

Once she stepped out of the wagon and into her own driveway, she was no longer in need of her aunt's assistance. After Margaret drove away, she went inside and immediately started getting her life back. First were the necessary calls to "reverse" her death, and with a little quibbling and a lot of paperwork, her checking accounts and credit cards were reactivated and her utilities were turned back on. Then she cleaned the house from top to bottom to rid it of three years' worth of dust.

After that was done, Adrienne was left with the daunting task of starting her new life back in Milwaukee.

She supposed she should look for a job, but her heart just wasn't in it. She'd gone to school and worked hard to be a fashion designer. She could easily pick up seasonal work with Thanksgiving days away and Christmas quick on its heels, but selling clothes at the mall for minimum wage seemed like a waste. Adrienne wasn't broke now that she could access her money. A month's worth of living expenses in Manhattan could keep her for three or four in Wisconsin, where her house was paid off and her car was almost too old to insure.

Looking at what she had, she decided to put off the inevitable for two months to let herself get acclimated and work through the crippling emotions that slowed most of her activities to a crawl. She would lose any job she got if she stopped folding clothes and started to randomly cry in the middle of the store. And there was still the risk of that. At first, she thought she'd shed every tear she could for Will Taylor in the private roomette headed for home. But every now and then her mind would stray and the pain in her chest would grow so acute that the only thing to relieve the pressure was more tears.

To combat it, she kept herself busy. If she couldn't think of Will, she couldn't wallow in the grief of everything she lost. The boxes she'd shipped from Manhattan before her flight were sitting in the living room, untouched. Inside were all the unsold clothes she'd designed for her boutique. She carried each piece upstairs to her mother's old sewing room and hung them on the large aluminum clothing rack.

This, she decided, would be her new workroom. It already had most of the supplies she needed from the days she'd spent working on things in high school and during breaks from college. Using her mother's old sewing machine had always seemed to bring her luck and motivation.

Really, just sitting in the room where her mother worked was inspirational to her. The collection she began at the apartment with Will came to an end as quickly as their relationship. She knew she needed to do something different. Adrienne needed an outlet for all her emotional energy, and the new pieces she envisioned in her mind would be it. Her work was often the best therapy. It had gotten her through her father's fatal heart attack several years back, and it could get her through this.

Gathering up her papers and pencils, she sat down at the worn dining room table and started designing a new collection. One that would remind her of the happy times she spent with Will before everything went wrong.

The color palate was easy to determine. There were a couple blouses and skirts in the warm fall colors of their walk through Central Park. A burgundy leather jacket with dark brown palazzo pants that reminded her of the décor of the Italian restaurant where they had their first date. To accent the collection, a short, sassy sweater-dress in the shade of the pale pink roses he brought her. Then, as a finale piece, a full-length gown in the same soft, blue-gray color as Will's eyes.

It took her days. She even worked through Thanksgiving without realizing it because her aunt never called to invite her over. When it was done, she had a stunning thirty-piece collection ready and waiting for her to bring it to life on the dress form. A mountain of fabric dominated the floor of her living room in anticipation of weeks of construction.

In time, Adrienne had fairly successfully buried her grief in her work. The pain of losing Will had faded to a dull ache she'd learned to ignore until she lay alone and cold in her bed each night.

When the phone rang one afternoon, she was busy at the sewing machine. She wasn't prone to get many calls, so she ran to the cordless and answered, breathless. "Hello?"

"Hello. Am I speaking with Adrienne Lockhart?"

"Yes," Adrienne sighed. The woman's voice sounded familiar, but the odds were that it was a reporter who'd been in touch calling back for more details to add to her feature. While most of her family and society had ignored her since she came home, she got the occasional phone call from reporters in New York who were writing about the mixup and the untimely demise of society darling Cynthia Dempsey. Adrienne usually had very little to say and told them she couldn't remember the weeks she'd lived as Cynthia. It was easier that way. She didn't want to say or do anything that might cause the Dempseys or Will any additional pain.

"Adrienne, this is Darlene Winters with *Trend Now* magazine. I don't know if you remember speaking to me at the party or not."

"I do, yes. It's so nice to speak with you again." *Nice* was an understatement. Her heart was pounding in her chest so loudly she almost couldn't hear the woman on the other end of the line. "I'm sorry I wasn't able to keep our appointment."

"Completely understandable, although it's the first time I've been stood up by someone who miraculously recovered from amnesia. I have to say it's a fascinating story. I've been following it in the papers."

Adrienne felt a touch of elation slip away. Was she just calling to use their acquaintance to get the inside scoop? "It isn't as interesting as it sounds."

"Honey, I saw you and Will Taylor dancing. You can tell the papers whatever you like, but I know a juicy story when I see one. But that's not why I'm calling."

Spying a nearby chair, Adrienne slumped down into it. If Darlene had good news for her, she wanted to be sitting down. Likewise if it was bad news.

"I know you probably think I was only interested in your work because of who I thought you were. I have a lot of young designers clamoring for my attention, so—true—it did make me take notice when I otherwise might not have. But I've found myself thinking about your designs since you've left. I never got to see the rest, and I'm quite disappointed."

Adrienne wasn't sure what to say. She'd FedEx Darlene whatever she wanted. All she had to do was ask. "I appreciate the interest. It's a huge compliment."

"You deserve it. Listen, are you aware of the charity work we do here at *Trend Now?*"

She was ashamed to admit she wasn't. "No, but I'd love to hear more about it."

"Well, every year around this time we put together a charity fashion show. All the proceeds go to support art and design education in our local public schools. It's called the Trend Next show to help us grow the next generation of fashion designers. In the show, we feature four up-and-coming designers. It's a smaller collection, ten looks from each one, but it's great exposure for them. After the show, we also select one designer to be featured in a five-page spread in *Trend Now*."

It was a good thing she was sitting down. The pounding of her heart had stopped along with her breathing. She was frozen stone-still, waiting for Darlene to say the magic words. She had to say them. There was no other reason for her to call, right? That would just be cruel.

"We usually make our selections months in advance to give the designers time to work. But this year, one of our designers has fallen seriously ill and had to drop out of the show. I know it's short notice, but I wanted to offer you the chance to take his place."

"Yes," she said without hesitation.

Darlene stumbled for a moment over her sudden response. "Are you sure? It's in two we—"

"Yes," she interrupted. "It could be tomorrow and I'd say yes."

"Well, all right, then. I'll have my office overnight you all the show's information and paperwork you need to sign. The show will be Saturday the fifteenth, so I'll see you there with your ten fiercest looks."

"Thank you for this opportunity, Darlene."

"Knock 'em dead. Bye, now."

The phone sat silent in Adrienne's hand, but she couldn't move her thumb to hang up. She was showing in New York at an event sponsored by one of the biggest fashion magazines in the world. The exposure potential was incredible. And if her collection were chosen for the magazine…

Perhaps her career wasn't over quite yet. Maybe the pain and suffering of surgeries, fractured bones, broken hearts and shattered dreams would be worth it if in the end she could make something of the mess.

Adrienne hurried downstairs to the dining room, where her sketches were scattered across the table. There were thirty designs and not a single one existed off the page yet. She could work in some of the pieces she'd already made, but it might not be cohesive enough. She started sorting though, axing the labor-intensive knitwear and pulling out the ten items she thought would make the most impact, the last being the blue satin gown. Even ten pieces would be a challenge. It would mean working nonstop for two solid weeks, but she would do it.

She had to.

"Mr. Taylor?" His assistant, Jeanine, popped her head into Will's office. "Mr. Dempsey is here to see you."

Frowning, Will took a big sip of his coffee. He figured eventually it would come around to this meeting. The one where the e-reader deal would finally fall through. He'd managed to avoid George for a few weeks, probably because George was avoiding him, too. They'd seen each other at Cynthia's funeral, but, unexpectedly, it had turned into a circus.

Cynthia's lover had shown up, wailing and throwing himself over her casket. It hadn't taken long for people to figure out who he was and turn to Will with mixed expressions of bewilderment and pity. George and Pauline were horrified by the scene, but her father, at least, didn't look surprised. Apparently the deteriorating state of their relationship was public knowledge, despite how hard he'd tried to hide it.

After that debacle, Will had buried himself in work and Thanksgiving festivities with his family. But now all that was behind them. There was nothing but frantic Christmas shopping over the next few weeks, of which he was sure George Dempsey did very little.

"Send him in."

George came through the door, his suit looking a little larger than normal on him. The man was in his sixties, but today was the first time Will had ever thought about his age. He looked every year and maybe a few more. He had bags under his eyes, his wrinkles were more prominent with the loss of some weight, probably due to stress. Losing Cynthia must've taken a larger toll on him than Will had imagined.

"George, please, sit down."

With a curt nod, George settled into a chair. "How are you faring, Will?"

Truth be told, he was miserable, but not because of Cynthia's death. His feelings for her had died long before she did. But he did feel horrible about her death. No one deserved to die like that.

"I'm hanging in there. I think it's going to be a struggle to get through the holidays."

George nodded. "Pauline doesn't quite know what to do with herself. She started to decorate for Christmas, then kept having to stop because she'd run across something that reminded her of Cynthia and she'd start crying. Cynthia was always so busy, it just seems like she's working late and will call any time now. Then you remember again."

Will understood the feeling. His apartment had been a ghost town. He kept walking into his place at night expecting Adrienne to be there. To hear the excited thumps of her bare feet as she ran to greet him at the door. To see her sitting at the kitchen table with toast and tea. He had very quickly gotten used to having her there with him.

"I've been doing a lot of thinking, Will." George eased back in his chair. "This e-reader project we've been working on has a lot of potential."

Which is why I've decided to sell to the highest bidder and you're out, Taylor.

"Which is why I've decided we should go forward with it."

Will's eyebrows shot up, his surprise plainly obvious to anyone who chose to look. "What about blood and family and all that?"

George shrugged. "Cynthia is dead, Will. Emma is sixteen, and I'm not about to marry her off to seal this deal. As much as I like working with family, there's no one I know that can make this as big a success as you can. This is the technology of now. It needs to go forward. We've got everything in place to do that."

Will wasn't quite sure what to say. George had been adamant about this from the beginning. The turn of events was surprising, to say the least. "Thank you, sir. I'm glad to hear you're still interested in working with us."

"I am because you're a good guy, Will. You stuck it out with Cynthia and took care of her even when you and I both know you were on the way out. Then you tried again to make it work, even if it was with the wrong woman. That's the kind of dedication and loyalty I look for in a business partner." He paused, his expression softening in a way Will had never seen before. "You were almost my son, Will. And that's good enough for me."

Flustered wasn't even the right word to describe Will's state of mind, but he held it together. They chatted for a while about trivial things. Then he thanked George, promised to have his office send over the final paperwork later in the week and walked him out.

The rush of success-fueled adrenaline shot through his veins as if he'd been pulled back from a precipice. He knew this project was going to launch the *Observer* into the same peer group as the *Times*. He could feel it in his bones.

Will wanted to celebrate but slumped back into his chair

instead. The victory was sadly hollow without Adrienne there to celebrate with him. Despite the suspicion and pain he couldn't put aside, when it came down to it, she was the one he wanted to kiss and take out for a night on the town with endless champagne. And she was gone.

Suddenly Will's tie felt too tight.

His office had been his retreat since Adrienne left. He'd worked more hours than ever, avoiding their empty home and the feelings he couldn't face. Now the walls of his spacious office were closing in on him. He didn't want to be here a second longer. Without even shutting down his laptop, he got up from his desk and walked out.

"Mr. Taylor?" Jeanine questioned when he started down the hallway.

"I'm going home. Reschedule anything on my calendar. Dan's in charge."

Will didn't wait for her response. He didn't want to be here right now. He hailed a cab on the curb and headed back to the apartment.

When he finally walked in the door, he had his mail clutched in one hand and his overcoat thrown over his arm. He stood in the entryway, hoping the restricting feeling in his chest would abate now that he was away from work, but it didn't. And he knew why.

Frustrated, he yanked off his tie and tossed everything onto the bed as he entered the bedroom. The bed was made and had been since the day Adrienne left. Being in it without her had felt odd, so he'd returned to sleeping in the guest room.

Something felt off. He'd been fighting the feeling for weeks, but he was too stubborn and hurt to seriously consider what was really bothering him. Their fight in the bathroom kept replaying in his head each night as he tried to sleep. The expression of fear and heartache on her face. How she'd tried to explain something he hadn't wanted to hear.

He stopped outside of the master bedroom closet. He'd slammed the door shut in a fit of rage after Adrienne left the apartment and hadn't gone in there since then. Will hadn't gone into her workroom either. There were too many memories locked inside.

Twisting the knob, Will pulled open the door and walked in. The neatly hung rows of clothing were the same, the boxes of priceless footwear lined up as always. The only thing out of place was a piece of clothing on the floor. He bent down and scooped up the discarded blouse. Stitched into the collar was a tag that read Adrienne Lockhart Designs. Just as she'd tried to tell him.

A million curse words came to mind, all of them directed back at himself. He was a jackass. She'd tried to tell him that day, but he hadn't wanted to listen. He'd leapt to his own conclusions and pushed her way.

Why?

Because it was easier than admitting he'd let himself fall for her. Easier than admitting he'd made love to a woman he knew in his heart wasn't his fiancée. He got himself out of a sticky situation by making it all her fault.

Why had he immediately turned everything she said into a lie? She was in a plane crash and nearly killed. She went through hours of reconstructive surgery, weeks in the hospital. The poor woman's face had been smashed in so badly they couldn't tell her from another passenger, but somehow a head trauma severe enough to scramble her memory had seemed outlandish.

Perhaps she would've recovered earlier if she'd been exposed to things she knew. Maybe if her family and friends had come to the hospital things would've clicked sooner. But the problem was compounded by strangers and doctors insisting she was someone she wasn't.

Will should've spoken up instead of quietly, privately questioning every time she acted out of character. They could've cleared the whole thing up weeks ago. Saved himself the heartache. But then he would've missed out on the joy and passion, too.

He hadn't wanted to clear things up. He hadn't wanted the considerate, loving woman in his arms to get away. Things were better than they had ever been, and for once in his life, he just wanted to enjoy life.

But what was the point, when he just turned around and drove her off?

Will walked out of the closet and flopped down onto the mattress. He'd made a mess he had no clue how to fix. If he booked the next flight to Milwaukee and showed up at her door, she'd probably slam it in his face. That was what he deserved. That's practically what he'd done to her.

A shift of his weight sent a piece of his mail sliding to the floor. He bent to pick it up. It looked like a party invitation for something he wouldn't attend. He had a social pass this holiday, given most people would consider him to be in mourning. Or in hiding.

Tearing open the envelope, he realized it was his invitation to the annual Trend Next fashion show. Usually, he sent Cynthia with a check and stayed home. This year, he'd just mail the check direct. As Will tossed the card onto the bed, he noticed a tiny slip of paper floating to the floor. Curious, he picked it up to read it.

"Due to unforeseen circumstances, Nick Matteo is unable to show at this event. Designer Adrienne Lockhart will be showing in his place."

Will's jaw dropped. He never expected her to be back in New York so soon. And to be showing at the Trend Next fashion show…that was an incredible opportunity for her. And for him. He wouldn't go to Wisconsin. With only days before the show, she needed to focus on her work, not deal with the emotional upheaval of his arrival.

But after the show...

Will called the number on the invitation to RSVP. This year's check would be delivered personally.

Thirteen

"That's the wrong belt! Who put that on her?"

Adrienne dashed through the throngs of people to the line of models queued up to show her designs to the world. Whipping off one belt and replacing it with the cincher made from the same burgundy leather she'd used for a bomber jacket on another model, she took a step back and sighed in relief. That was close.

It had been absolute chaos for over three hours. The girls had to get their hair styled, their makeup done and get into their assigned clothes. Adrienne had to make sure each model had the proper accessories to finish off the look of each outfit. She was the last to go, so she'd seen how the other designers had handled their shows, but none of it could prepare her for her turn.

"Is everyone ready?"

After two weeks of working on a solid diet of caffeine, sugar and almost no sleep, she wasn't sure that she was. But ready or not, her chance had come. If she could make it through the next hour or so, she could sleep for a week to make up for it.

"Miss Lockhart, you're up." The production manager smiled and handed her a microphone. "Good luck."

Adrienne took a deep breath, straightened her own brown leather skirt and moss-green blouse, which was actually the eleventh look of the collection, and strode confidently out onto the catwalk.

It was nearly impossible to see the crowd. The bright stage lighting made her squint for a few seconds as her eyes adjusted. If not for the applause, she could have convinced herself there were only five people out there, which made the next part easier. She had never been good with public speaking. She was better behind a sewing machine, but this was part of the job.

When the applause finally quieted, she raised the microphone to her lips. "Good evening, everyone. My name is Adrienne Lockhart, and I'm thrilled to be sharing my work with you tonight. My collection was inspired by the almost unbelievable last few months I spent in New York. You might recognize my name from the local papers, but if you don't know, I'll fill you in. I almost died, got a new face, lost my memory, fell in love, fell out of love and finally found myself and my passion for designing again. Manhattan is a crazy town to get caught up in, and every moment of it is captured here tonight. I hope you enjoy it."

With a wave, Adrienne turned and disappeared around the corner, the wall muffling the sound of applause. As she passed off the microphone to a stage hand, the music she had selected for the show began. It was a beautiful melody with a heavy bass tempo for the models to stomp their hearts out to.

Before she could catch her breath, the first model took off and the show was on its way.

Here goes nothing.

She watched from a monitor backstage as each woman showcased the look she designed and selected for them. It was a parade of deep, rich tones, textures, fabrics and blood, sweat and tears. It was the perfect fall collection and the perfect reflection of her time with Will.

At last the finale dress was up. The blue-gray fit-and-flare organza gown was her crowning glory, a piece even more fabulous than the green dress she wore to her party. It was one-shouldered and gathered and draped tightly around the torso, exploding into a full, sweeping skirt that started just below the swell of the model's hips. She'd deliberately selected a fuller-figured model for this dress because breasts and hips were an absolute must for it to fit correctly.

Adrienne held her breath as the dress disappeared around the corner and all the other models lined back up for the final walk.

"Clapping and smiling, ladies," the production manager said as they started back down the catwalk. "That goes for you, too," he reminded Adrienne.

Pasting on a bright smile, she followed behind the ball gown, waving as the roar of applause nearly knocked her backward. She could still barely see the crowd with the bright lights, flashing cameras and the dark seating areas, but the sound they made as she came out was stunning.

This was her moment. Tears formed in her eyes as she took it all in, stopping at the end of the runway to give a short bow and blow a kiss to the audience. As she turned to follow the models backstage, she thought she caught a glimpse of someone familiar sitting in the front row.

It was just wishful thinking—her mind adding his face to another man's body because she wanted so badly to share this moment with him. Or maybe just tears mixing with spotlights to obscure her vision. There was no way Will Taylor was sitting in the front row of her fashion show holding a bundle of pale pink roses in his lap like the petal-colored fabric in her collection.

With a shake of her head to put the thought aside, she headed backstage and tried to focus on the joy. She wasn't about to let a mistaken Will sighting cause her to start moping and ruin this beautiful moment.

Fortunately, the chaos backstage pushed any remaining thoughts from her head. Models and designers were running around, and journalists and spectators were coming backstage to talk to people about the show. It made Adrienne wish she had someone here with her. Gwen had to work, and she hadn't felt comfortable inviting the Dempseys so soon after Cynthia's funeral. Unsure of what else to do, she returned to her staging area and started helping her models out of their outfits, hanging them back up neatly.

She was interrupted a few times by journalists asking questions. A couple wanted pictures, so she posed alone or with one or two of the models still wearing her designs.

"What was your inspiration for that beautiful blue gown?" one of them asked.

"That was the color of my lover's eyes," she said with a rueful smile. She'd searched through five fabric stores trying to find the perfect shade. Milwaukee didn't have anything as comprehensive as the shops in the Garment District.

The journalist wrote feverishly, took a few pictures and then disappeared to talk to someone else.

Before long the noise quieted, the models and journalists left and the designers and production workers began breaking down. Adrienne zipped up the side of the rolling garment armoire and scooped the last of the accessories into a drawstring bag she tied to the rack.

It was done. She'd nearly killed herself doing it, but she'd created a collection and had shown it on the catwalks of a Manhattan fashion show. If nothing else ever came of this night, she would be happy for this chance.

"Adrienne?" a woman's voice called, and she turned to see who was still hanging around. It was Darlene.

Adrienne didn't hesitate to give the woman a hug as she approached. "Thank you so much for this opportunity."

"Honey, thank *you*. When our fourth designer cancelled, I didn't know what I was going to do. You saved me, and you certainly didn't disappoint. Everyone is buzzing about your work. I think it was the best of the four."

"Really?" Adrienne had wanted to do a great job but figured that against designers with months to prepare, she'd do well just to not embarrass herself in front of the industry types.

"I was talking with Milton, the owner of *Trend Now,* and we both agree that your collection is the one we want to feature in the March issue. I just loved the leather, and that ball gown was divine."

Adrienne's mouth dropped open, appropriate words escaping her. "Are you serious?" was all she could come up with.

"Absolutely. I don't know how you did it, but the work was just outstanding. If you can stay in Manhattan through the week, we'll get the fashion shoot set up in a couple of days."

"Of course." Adrienne was staying with Gwen and had planned to hang around New York for a few days. She wanted to visit a couple friends from her pre-accident SoHo days and do some Christmas shopping. She always enjoyed the window displays and decorations that took over this time of year.

Adrienne handed Darlene one of her newly minted business cards with her cell phone number on it. "This is where you can reach me while I'm here."

"I'll call you tomorrow," she said. "Go out on the town and party tonight. You earned it."

She watched Darlene walk away. Once the fashion editor had disappeared around a corner, Adrienne flopped into one of the chairs at the makeup station. She was emotionally and physically spent, but she didn't care. She *did* have the talent to make it. Sometimes she wasn't certain, but validation couldn't come from a better source than Darlene. She didn't strike her as the kind to say great things when they weren't true. She wanted to sell magazines.

This might really turn things around for her. There was no way she could afford to open another shop, but maybe she could vamp up her website and send pieces to stylists who might actually use them in photo shoots for a change. Then maybe, just maybe, she could consider moving back and opening a storefront. Perhaps Gwen would be interested in sharing a two-bedroom place somewhere. Splitting rent would make life more livable.

"Are you planning on opening up a shop in Manhattan any time soon?" a familiar man's voice called to her, the deep tones echoing off the large empty space and concrete floors.

Her mind was playing tricks on her again. First she saw Will in the audience and then she heard his voice. It was going to take longer to get over him than she'd hoped. With a shake of her head, she turned in her chair and opened her mouth to answer, then stopped.

She wasn't crazy. Will was standing about ten feet away. He was looking more devastatingly handsome than ever, wearing jeans and a button-down shirt with a leather jacket over it instead of his standard suit. The angry expression she'd last seen on his face was gone, a bouquet of pink roses clutched in his hands.

Adrienne wouldn't allow herself to speculate on what his arrival, with flowers no less, meant. She'd survived a plane crash and managed to fulfill a lifelong dream. Certainly her string of luck was running out, especially where love was concerned. "No," she finally answered, standing to face him head-on. "As nice as this exposure is, I won't earn a dime off it if it doesn't build demand. I can't afford a store."

"That's a shame," he said. "I know a guy who has the perfect space for rent. He'd probably give you a great deal on it if you were interested."

Had he really come all the way down here to give her a tip on a real-estate opportunity? Apparently the roses meant very little. Just a gesture for her debut, she supposed. One of the other designers got flowers, too.

No matter how good the deal, she couldn't afford it, but she had to ask. "How great?"

"Free."

Adrienne shook her head and looked down at the square toes of her brown leather boots. "Nothing is free."

"Absolutely free," he insisted. "No strings attached."

He was just toying with her now, and it brought a surge of irritation through her body. The anger she couldn't express when he'd cast her aside rose to the surface, her cheeks getting warm and flush. "Why would he do that?"

"He doesn't need the money. And I think the owner feels badly about how things worked out for you."

Adrienne scoffed, crossing her arms protectively across her chest. "Things worked out great for me. I just had my first fashion show. I'm going to be featured in *Trend Now* magazine. My career is doing great. And you can tell '*him*' I don't need his pity offering. I'll get a place when I can afford to do it on my own."

Will's eyes widened at her angry outburst, and his brow furrowed in thought. This conversation obviously wasn't going the way he'd hoped. If he thought he could just march in here, offer her real estate and some roses and everything would be better between them, he was wrong. He'd broken her heart. Sent her out the door like a pesky vacuum salesman without a dollar in her pocket. She couldn't allow herself to trust someone who could turn on her so quickly. And there was no hope for love without trust. So what did they have left?

Nothing, it pained her to admit.

"When you came out before the show, you said that over the past few months you'd fallen in love. And out of it," he added with a slightly pained expression.

Adrienne had made that statement without thinking for a minute that Will would be in the audience. In truth, she did still love him. She ached to reach out and brush a stray strand of his hair from his forehead. She wanted to bury her face in his neck and cling to him so tightly he could never leave her again. But she wasn't stupid. The last time she was honest with him, he stomped on her heart. Will was a strategist, a businessman. She couldn't let him have the upper hand this time.

"So?" she challenged.

"So," he said, taking a few steps closer, "I wanted to know if that was true. Have you fallen out of love with me?"

Adrienne looked up, the most defiant expression she could muster plastered on her face. She wasn't about to fly into his arms and confess her love just to get cast aside again. "It is true," she lied. "I don't love you anymore, Will Taylor."

Will tried not to smile. He'd lied when he walked out of the hospital room that day. Adrienne was the worst actress ever. She couldn't lie her way out of a paper bag, much less feign almost two months of amnesia. No way she could be the master of deception he'd accused her of being.

But more important, she was lying now. She still loved him. He was certain of it. She just wasn't going to admit it. Will understood. He had hurt her, betrayed her. He knew how that felt. He didn't deserve her love, but he wanted it anyway. He just had to get her to admit it.

"I'm sorry you feel that way," he said.

"You broke my heart, and I'm not about to trust you with it again." Adrienne's voice trembled slightly as she spoke. He knew how hard it had to be for her to say that, especially knowing she did care for him. She was still his fighter.

Will nodded. "I'd like to help fix what I've ruined, but I understand if you're not interested. It's a shame, though," he said, taking half a step backward.

"Why's that?" she asked, moving forward as he moved back.

He could tell she was putting up a brave face but wasn't ready for him to walk away just yet. "Well, you see, the man is friends with a real-estate developer and got talked into investing in some property, but he's very particular about who he rents to. He's head over heels in love with a woman, but if she doesn't want the shop and doesn't want him, he'll be forced to lease it out to some overpriced teenage outlet."

"No!" she said, reaching out with a look of panic on her face.

"No, what?" he pressed, seeing the crack in her stern façade. "No, you want the store? No, you want me? Or no, don't rent it to a chain store?"

Adrienne shook her head, the fight abandoning her. "No to all of it."

Will slowly closed the gap between them and held out the flowers. "I brought these for you."

She accepted them, taking a deep breath of their fragrance. "Thank you."

"I'm sorry for how I acted. I'm sorry for not believing you. I was having trouble dealing with all of this, with how I felt about you and Cynthia, and I took it out on you."

She looked up at him, her expression open but not entirely sold. The flowers had been a nice touch, but they hadn't quite worked the magic he was hoping for. He'd have to take it up a notch. "The other day George came by the office and agreed on the e-reader deal. It took years of long hours to pull that together, and it meant nothing because I couldn't share the moment with you. Not Cynthia. *You*. Adrienne. In that short period of time, you became more important to me than anything. Than anyone."

She still didn't speak, but her gaze dropped to the roses, her knuckles gripping the stems and turning white with strain.

He moved in closer, bringing his hands up to gently hold the backs of her upper arms. He wasn't about to let her get away. "I know that I was horrible to you. And I don't deserve your forgiveness. But I'm asking for it. Because I love you, Adrienne. I've never felt this way about anyone before, and frankly, it scared me. But those weeks without you were like living with a part of me missing. And even if I can't have you, if I've ruined it, I couldn't bear to know you hated me."

He tilted Adrienne's chin up to look at him, and he saw the tears swimming in her green-gold eyes.

"I don't hate you," she whispered, trying to look away, but he wouldn't let her.

"But do you still love me?" he pressed.

"Yes." She nodded, a tear escaping and rolling down her cheek. "I love you, Will."

He took the roses from her, threw them onto one of the dressing tables and pulled her into his embrace, nearly crushing her against his chest. Will buried his face into the naturally kinky waves of her chestnut hair and breathed in the scent he'd missed.

"I'm so glad I didn't ruin it," he said, pulling away. "I was hopeful, though, so I brought this with me just in case."

Will took a box out of his pocket and eased down onto one knee in front of her. He watched with amusement and a touch of concern as the blood drained from her face. He wasn't sure if that was good or bad.

He held up the box to her. "Open it," he urged.

Adrienne reached out, her hand shaking, and took the velvet box. She opened it, her mouth dropping open as it tended to do when she wasn't sure what to say.

"It's not the same ring," she said, her brow furrowed.

It wasn't. It felt wrong to give her a ring that was intended for someone else. So he'd gone to his favorite jeweler and asked him to create a new ring especially for Adrienne.

It was a two-carat oval-cut pink sapphire surrounded by a ring of perfect, round diamonds and set in platinum. The jeweler was inspired by Princess Diana's engagement ring, recently given by her son to the new English princess.

Judging by the look on Adrienne's face, he'd made the right choice.

"Cynthia's ring was large and gaudy because that's what she wanted. I wanted your ring to be untraditional, beautiful and priceless. Just like you."

Will pulled the ring from the box and slipped it onto her finger. It fit perfectly, unlike all of Cynthia's things. This was hers and only hers.

"Adrienne, you have changed my whole world. I had been living half a life before you were given to me. Just going through the motions. I'd lost hope of ever being happy. But I was wrong. You showed me there was more to life than how I was living. You made me want to do and experience more through your eyes. And I want to continue to do that. For the rest of our lives. Marry me, Adrienne."

She dropped to her knees on the ground in front on him. Her eyes moved repeatedly from the ring to his face and back. "It's so beautiful. I don't know what to say, Will."

Will smiled and took her hands in his. "All you have to say is yes."

"Yes!" she said, launching herself into his arms. His weight was thrown off by the sudden attack, sending him rolling backward onto the concrete floor with Adrienne on top of him.

She straddled him, leaning down to put her palms on each side of his face, and kissed him. Will wrapped his arms around her and held her tight against him. It felt so good to have her back in his embrace again. He'd missed holding her so badly the past few weeks. His arms were empty and use-less without her.

When his lips finally parted from hers, he took a ragged breath to cool his ardor. This was hardly the time or place for him to do everything he wanted to do to his new fiancée.

He was distracted as Adrienne started giggling.

"What?" he asked. One moment she was mad, then crying, then laughing. She would definitely keep him on his toes for the next fifty years.

"We're getting married," Adrienne said, as though he hadn't been present to hear the news.

"I know." Will pushed himself up until he was seated on the floor with Adrienne in his lap, her legs wrapped around his waist. "Does that mean you'll move back to New York and live with me?"

Adrienne nodded. "I have to go home and take care of some things, but it won't take me long. But if I do move back here, I want us to start fresh with a line separating our new life together from the past. I think the best way to do it would be to get a new apartment. Can we?"

"Absolutely." Will smiled. He'd been looking at places on the Upper West Side already. It was closer to the office, and the pace had always suited him better.

"And can we get new furniture? Stuff that isn't so…I don't know…"

"I *do* know." He laughed. He hated almost everything in that place. "And we can most definitely start over with deco-rating. We'll have an estate sale and only take what we want."

"Like my sewing machine." Adrienne grinned, the excite-ment of their new life together visibly forming in her mind. "I guess there's just one thing left to discuss."

"Ahh…here we go. The wedding plans, right? Let the circus begin."

Will didn't know what Adrienne's take on the wedding might be like, but he was certain it would be different, just like their life together would be different. And wonderful. And exciting. He couldn't wait to find out what their future would hold.

"Whatever you want, we can make it happen. I'll track down every pink rose in South America if you want it. Anything for you."

Adrienne smiled sheepishly. "That's wonderful, thank you. But actually, that's not what I was talking about."

Will arched an eyebrow in curiosity. She surprised him all the time. He'd proposed not two minutes ago. He figured her head would at least be wrapped up in designing her own wedding gown and bridesmaids dresses if not envisioning the whole extravaganza. "So, what's more important than planning our wedding?"

"You said something earlier about a rent-free location for my new boutique?"

Epilogue

The Daily Observer, Society Column
By Annabelle Reed-Graham
Saturday, October Twentieth
Central Park

I'm certain that all of my readers have been following the real-life drama over the last year that has been the romance of *Daily Observer* mogul (and my boss) William Reese Taylor, III, and his fiancée, the beautiful and talented fashion designer Adrienne Lockhart. I've been personally cheering for the couple through the ups and downs and have never been as excited to type an engagement announcement as I was this past December when the groom proposed with a flawless pink-sapphire-and-diamond ring reminiscent of the jewels of royalty. I've waited months with bated breath, but this past weekend, I had the privilege of attending their intimate autumn wedding.

For those of you expecting one of those large, stuffy and

expensive extravaganzas at the Plaza, you're in for a big surprise. While the bride's funky fashion sense and free spirit are well known, no one was quite certain how the event would unfold. Guesses ranged from hot-pink wedding gowns to a ceremony on a rooftop, but we were all wrong. What resulted was a beautifully traditional event with customized elements that made this wedding uniquely their own.

The wedding ceremony took place in Central Park's Shakespeare Gardens, where a gathering of less than a hundred close friends and family members joined the bride and groom in celebrating their vows. The guests were serenaded by an elegant string quartet while they waited for the bride's arrival.

To everyone's surprise, the bride was walked down the aisle by George Dempsey, the owner of Dempsey Corp. and father of the late Cynthia Dempsey. The bride looked stunning in an ivory satin-and-organza gown, which she designed herself. The strapless dress had a corset top, studded with hand-sewn pearls and gold and silver Swarovski crystals set in a mystical swirling pattern across the bodice. The skirt was full and voluminous, swishing around the blushing bride like a bell. If you looked closely, you could catch a glimpse of the cheeky ivory and crystal flip-flop sandals she wore underneath it.

The flowers were expertly handled by Chestnuts in the Tuileries. The bride's bouquet was a tight bundle of ivory roses with pink tips and stephanotis with pink crystal centers. The petal-pink ribbon around the stems matched the gown of the maid of honor, Miss Gwendolyn Wright, a friend of the bride and nurse at the hospital where the bride stayed after her tragic accident a year ago.

The groom and his best man, Mr. Alexander Stanton, both looked fetching in their Armani tuxedos. There wasn't an ounce of nervousness in the groom. In fact, his gaze was focused so intently on his new bride as she walked down the petal-strewn aisle, the rest of us could've gone home and he wouldn't have noticed.

The bride and groom exchanged customized vows under an arch woven with white hydrangeas and pink and ivory roses. I've personally written about more than a hundred weddings over the years, and I have to say I've never seen a couple beaming with as much love and joy as they did pledging their devotion to one another.

After the ceremony, guests were treated to a horse-drawn-carriage ride around Central Park to the Loeb Boathouse, where the reception was held. Guests sipped the night's signature cocktail, "The Barefoot Bride," a concoction of vodka, pureed strawberries and lemon seltzer, and dined on fun, nontraditional treats like filet mignon sliders, fried macaroni-and-cheese spoons and miniature corn dogs served in shot glasses with spicy Chinese mustard.

The warm wood tones of the rustic but elegant Boathouse were the perfect backdrop to the cream, rose and gold decorations. The walls were lit up in a delicate pink light, and each surface was covered in staggered sizes of ivory pillar candles and pink rose petals. Each guest table was draped with custom, hand-stitched rose-colored linens, embroidered with tiny pearls and crystals in the same swirling pattern as the bride's gown. The glow of more ivory candles highlighted the four-foot-tall gold trumpet vases overflowing with more roses, lilies and hydrangeas and dripping with strands of crystals and pearls.

When the wedding party arrived, the bride and groom shared a lively first dance to the unexpected "Never Can Tell" by Chuck Berry. They were later joined on the dance floor by the maid of honor and best man. Once the tempo of the music dropped, I have to admit I sensed something romantic happening between those two. Something to keep an eye on, since the best man is a notorious playboy.

The event was a feast for all five senses. After the first few dances, guests were treated to a gourmet meal that included a strawberry spinach salad, cold melon soup and a tender filet with shrimp, garlic whipped potatoes and roasted asparagus.

True to the bride's style, the wedding cake was a fun and funky creation from local bakery Cake Alchemy. Forgoing the traditional sugar flowers, the square-tiered fondant cake was decorated with a cascade of pink, ivory and burgundy blown sugar globes. The four-foot creation featured alternating tiers of black-forest cake with cherry and cream filling and white-chocolate cake with fresh strawberry-buttercream filling.

After dinner, the bride reappeared in a shimmering, cocktail-length fuchsia gown of her own design, and a swing band kept guests dancing late into the night. As the cocktail foretold, the bride and many of the ladies attending cast aside their shoes to dance barefoot on the seamless white dance floor, illuminated with the bride and groom's initials.

Attendees who overheated had the option of relaxing on the pier, taking a trip around the lake in specially reserved gondolas or indulging in the late-night appearance of a make-your-own-sundae bar. It was a much appreciated treat after a long evening of wedding celebration. I personally opted for caramel and candied pecans with a creamy French-vanilla ice cream, but the choices were endless.

Upon departure, each lady was provided with a silk drawstring satchel and each gentleman an embroidered handkerchief by Adrienne Lockhart Designs. Inside the purses, they found a card telling them that a donation had been made in their name to the Trend Next Foundation, the same organization that helped launch the bride's successful career last year.

Before leaving, I had the opportunity to speak with the happy couple. I asked them, as I ask all my brides and grooms, what their wishes for the future were.

"My wish," the bride said, "is that we can spend every day

of the next fifty years as happy and in love as we are at this exact moment."

"Make it sixty years," the groom replied, sweeping the bride into a toe-curling kiss that brought a blush to this old biddy's cheeks.

I have to admit, watching the couple depart the Boathouse for their own horse-drawn carriage amongst the twinkling of sparklers, I got a little teary eyed. I hope the new Mr. and Mrs. William Reese Taylor, III, remain this blissfully happy forever. I've never met a couple who deserves it more.

* * * * *

PASSION

COMING NEXT MONTH
AVAILABLE MAY 8, 2012

#2155 UNDONE BY HER TENDER TOUCH
Pregnancy & Passion
Maya Banks
When one night with magnate Cam Hollingsworth results in pregnancy, no-strings-attached turns into a tangled web for caterer Pippa Laingley.

#2156 ONE DANCE WITH THE SHEIKH
Dynasties: The Kincaids
Tessa Radley

#2157 THE TIES THAT BIND
Billionaires and Babies
Emilie Rose

#2158 AN INTIMATE BARGAIN
Colorado Cattle Barons
Barbara Dunlop

#2159 RELENTLESS PURSUIT
Lone Star Legacy
Sara Orwig

#2160 READY FOR HER CLOSE-UP
Matchmakers, Inc.
Katherine Garbera

REQUEST YOUR FREE BOOKS!
2 FREE NOVELS PLUS 2 FREE GIFTS!

Harlequin®

Desire

ALWAYS POWERFUL, PASSIONATE AND PROVOCATIVE

YES! Please send me 2 FREE Harlequin Desire® novels and my 2 FREE gifts (gifts are worth about $10). After receiving them, if I don't wish to receive any more books, I can return the shipping statement marked "cancel." If I don't cancel, I will receive 6 brand-new novels every month and be billed just $4.30 per book in the U.S. or $4.99 per book in Canada. That's a saving of at least 14% off the cover price! It's quite a bargain! Shipping and handling is just 50¢ per book in the U.S. and 75¢ per book in Canada.* I understand that accepting the 2 free books and gifts places me under no obligation to buy anything. I can always return a shipment and cancel at any time. Even if I never buy another book, the two free books and gifts are mine to keep forever.

225/326 HDN FEF3

Name _____ (PLEASE PRINT)

Address _____ Apt. #

City _____ State/Prov. _____ Zip/Postal Code

Signature (if under 18, a parent or guardian must sign)

Mail to the **Reader Service:**
IN U.S.A.: P.O. Box 1867, Buffalo, NY 14240-1867
IN CANADA: P.O. Box 609, Fort Erie, Ontario L2A 5X3

Not valid for current subscribers to Harlequin Desire books.

Want to try two free books from another line?
Call 1-800-873-8635 or visit www.ReaderService.com.

* Terms and prices subject to change without notice. Prices do not include applicable taxes. Sales tax applicable in N.Y. Canadian residents will be charged applicable taxes. Offer not valid in Quebec. This offer is limited to one order per household. All orders subject to credit approval. Credit or debit balances in a customer's account(s) may be offset by any other outstanding balance owed by or to the customer. Please allow 4 to 6 weeks for delivery. Offer available while quantities last.

Your Privacy—The Reader Service is committed to protecting your privacy. Our Privacy Policy is available online at www.ReaderService.com or upon request from the Reader Service.

We make a portion of our mailing list available to reputable third parties that offer products we believe may interest you. If you prefer that we not exchange your name with third parties, or if you wish to clarify or modify your communication preferences, please visit us at www.ReaderService.com/consumerschoice or write to us at Reader Service Preference Service, P.O. Box 9062, Buffalo, NY 14269. Include your complete name and address.

HDES11B

New York Times *and* USA TODAY *bestselling author*
Maya Banks presents book four in her miniseries
PREGNANCY & PASSION

UNDONE BY HER TENDER TOUCH

Available May 2012 from Harlequin® Desire!

"**W**ould you like some help?"

Pippa whirled around, still holding the bottle of champagne, and darn near tossed the contents onto the floor.

"Help?"

Cam nodded slowly. "Assistance? You look as though you could use it. How on earth did you think you'd manage to cater this event on your own?"

Pippa was horrified by his offer and then, as she processed the rest of his statement, she was irritated as hell.

"I'd hate for you to sully those pretty hands," she snapped. "And for your information, I've got this under control. The help didn't show. Not my fault. The food is impeccable, if I do say so myself. I just need to deliver it to the guests."

"I believe I just offered my assistance and you insulted me," Cam said dryly.

Her eyebrows drew together. Oh, why did the man have to be so damn delicious-looking? And why could she never perform the simplest functions around him?

"You're Ashley's guest," Pippa said firmly. "Not to mention you're used to being served, not serving others."

"How do you know what I'm used to?" he asked mildly.

She had absolutely nothing to say to that and watched in bewilderment as he hefted the tray up and walked out of the kitchen.

She sagged against the sink, her pulse racing hard enough

to make her dizzy.

Cameron Hollingsworth was gorgeous, unpolished in a rough and totally sexy way, arrogant and so wrong for her. But there was something about the man that just did it for her.

She sighed. He was a luscious specimen of a male and he couldn't be any less interested in her.

Even so, she was itching to shake his world up a little.

Realizing she was spending far too much time mooning over Cameron, she grabbed another tray, took a deep breath to compose herself and then headed toward the living room.

And Cameron Hollingsworth.

Will Pippa shake up Cameron's world?
Find out in Maya Banks's passionate new novel

UNDONE BY HER TENDER TOUCH

Available May 2012 from Harlequin® Desire!

Harlequin *Presents*

Royalty has never been so scandalous!

When Crown Prince Alessandro of Santina proposes
to paparazzi favorite Allegra Jackson it promises
to be *the* social event of the decade!

Harlequin Presents® invites you to step into the decadent
playground of the world's rich and famous and rub shoulders
with royalty, sheikhs and glamorous socialites.

**Collect all 8 passionate tales written by *USA TODAY*
bestselling authors, beginning May 2012!**